Anyone but Alex

THE ENGLISH BROTHERS, BOOK #3
THE BLUEBERRY LANE SERIES

KATY REGNERY

SPENCER
HILL
PRESS

Please visit www.katyregnery.com

First Edition: September 2014
Katy Regnery

Anyone but Alex : a novel / by Katy Regnery—1st ed.
ISBN: 978-1-63392-074-3

Library of Congress Cataloging-in-Publication Data available upon request

Published in the United States by Spencer Hill Press
This is a Spencer Hill Contemporary Romance, Spencer Hill
Contemporary is an imprint of Spencer Hill Press.
For more information on our titles visit www.spencerhillpress.com

Distributed by Midpoint Trade Books
www.midpointtrade.com

Cover design by: Marianne Nowicki
Interior layout by: Scribe Inc.
The World of Blueberry Lane Map designed by: Paul Siegel

Printed in the United States of America

The Blueberry Lane Series

THE ENGLISH BROTHERS
Breaking Up with Barrett
Falling for Fitz
Anyone but Alex
Seduced by Stratton
Wild about Weston
Kiss Me Kate
Marrying Mr. English

THE WINSLOW BROTHERS
Bidding on Brooks
Proposing to Preston
Crazy about Cameron
Campaigning for Christopher

THE ROUSSEAUS
Jonquils for Jax
Coming August 2016

Marry Me Mad
Coming September 2016

J.C. and the Bijoux Jolis
Coming October 2016

THE STORY SISTERS
Four novels
Coming 2017

THE AMBLERS
Three novels
Coming 2018

Based on the best-selling series by Katy Regnery,

The World of...

The Rousseaus of Chateau Nouvelle
Jax, Mad, J.C.
Jonquils for Jax • Marry Me Mad
J.C and the Bijoux Jolis

The Story Sisters of Forrester
Priscilla, Alice, Elizabeth, Jane
Coming Summer 2017

The Winslow Brothers of Westerly
Brooks, Preston, Cameron, Christopher
Bidding on Brooks • Proposing to Preston
Crazy About Cameron • Campaigning for Christopher

The Amblers of Greens Farms
Bree, Dash, Sloane
Coming Summer 2018

The English Brothers of Haverford Park
Barrett, Fitz, Alex, Stratton, Weston, Kate
Breaking up with Barrett • Falling for Fitz
Anyone but Alex • Seduced by Stratton
Wild about Weston • Kiss Me Kate
Marrying Mr. English

For Henry and Callie, who love it when
Mommy dedicates one of her books to them.
Henry, don't ever be an Alex.
And Callie, don't ever fall for one.

CONTENTS

Chapter 1

There was something wrong with Alex English.

During his standing date with Hope Atwell in a deluxe suite at the Four Seasons Hotel last Thursday, he had to force himself to concentrate on the task at hand. While he grasped Hope's bare hips and thrust into her from behind over and over again, his thoughts drifted to work, to friends, to his family, to the Eagles, to the room decor . . . for God's sake. Bored by her predictable moans and vulgar compliments, he closed his eyes and finished the deed, but the entire act left him feeling unsatisfied. Annoyed by Hope's banal postcoital conversation, Alex used a nonexistent work meeting as an excuse to leave her, and returned to the office.

At a birthday party last Friday night, Alex renewed his acquaintance with Juliette Dunne, with whom he had brokered two big deals last year and enjoyed memorable sex on top of the boardroom table at English & Sons to celebrate. After flirting with her for most of the night, he'd followed her home, only to find himself distracted again. As Juliette whimpered, "Oh God. Oh God. *OhGodOhGodOhGod*," taking a million years to climax, Alex wondered if it would be rude for him to go ahead and finish without her, because aside from the reliable physical rush he got from screwing someone, he wasn't feeling much else. After she'd finally yowled her way through an orgasm, Alex quickly climaxed, but again, he was left feeling empty.

Feeling a woman shudder and tremble around him, calling his name and clawing her way down his back usually made Alex feel like the king of the world. Sated and limp, he'd contently stroke a woman's naked back for hours while she prattled on about her life, about her horses or kids or boss or backhand, waiting for an appropriate amount of time to pass before flipping her over and having her again. He had fun, she had fun, and after brunch the next morning and a long, sloppy, lingering kiss good-bye, he'd head for home with a bounce in his step, his mind already turning to his next rendezvous.

But his chest literally ached as he lay beside Juliette, who started talking about her latest deal. Numbers-while-naked should have been enough to make Alex instantly hard again, but all he felt was desperate to leave. Making the excuse of walking a dog he didn't actually have, Alex skipped out of Juliette's apartment at midnight and headed home alone.

Hoping to remedy the problem, Alex had ramped up his frequency and varied his partners the following week, adding—in addition to Hope—a tennis pro from the club, a hot cocktail waitress from his favorite hotel, a Junior League fund-raiser type whose husband was in Paris, and a Manhattan fashion model doing a photo shoot at the LOVE sculpture. All were beautiful. All were enthusiastic, compliant, and willing, and as an added bonus, the fashion model was surprisingly flexible.

The "something wrong" with Alex English?

Each and every time, after the deed was done, Alex didn't feel satisfaction or contentment or peace. He felt so hollow, it was painful, and it was genuinely starting to worry him.

At twenty-nine years old, Alex had enjoyed a solid fourteen years of getting whatever piece of ass he wanted, whenever he wanted it. And Alex had wanted it all the time. Young women, older women, married, unmarried, beautiful, plain, brunette, blonde, filthy, virginal, rough, and meek: he'd enjoyed them all ten different ways from Saturday and once more on Sunday morning before taking them to brunch. His reputation was infamous, and he'd heard every variation on his character: Casanova, Don Juan, manwhore, womanizer, heartbreaker, and among his friends? The Professor. Casual sex was Alex's forte, his living room, his favorite. He had no trouble procuring it, he performed like a god, and it always left him feeling awesome.

Until now.

After yet another lackluster date with Hope at the Four Seasons, Alex gave the matter some serious thought as he walked back to the office. He had hurt Hope's feelings this week—he could see the confused disappointment in her eyes when he left, after climaxing before *and* without her, then rolling quickly away. He'd made an excuse about work and kissed her farewell, but he couldn't get away from her fast enough—the emptiness turning to panic as he realized that this problem wasn't just going to go away by bedding more women. If anything, it was only getting worse.

As Alex walked the dozen blocks back to his office, he was shocked to realize that he could actually pinpoint the moment his troubles had started.

When his older brothers, Barrett and Fitz, had gotten engaged a month ago, as he watched Barrett with Emily, Fitz with Daisy, something happened inside Alex. His chest had started to ache. The pain was so sharp and unexpected, in fact, that as his father had uncorked a bottle of champagne to celebrate the engagements, Alex had slipped unnoticed from the living room to collect his thoughts outside. As he stood on the west terrace in the moonlight, palm pressed against his chest, sucking down gulps of cold, fresh air, he'd managed to convince himself that the ache was nothing more than some indigestion from the raw cheese his mother liked to serve with cocktails. It had nothing to do with Barrett and Fitz falling in love. He had rubbed his chest until the ache dulled to bearable, pasted a smile on his face, and returned in time for toasts.

But in the morning, the ache hadn't gone away, and its source was elusive and just out of reach. As the weeks went by, he realized it was a constant longing in the pit of his stomach, an emptiness that no amount of sex could fill, made fathomless by his efforts. He didn't have a name for it, but he hated the way it made him feel. Worse, he hated the way it was starting to affect his sex life. For the first time Alex could remember, sex on its own wasn't enough. He wanted—no, he *needed*—something more.

This frustrated him mightily because all he *wanted* was to get his life back to the way it was: regular, *satisfying*, casual sex with an oysterful of gorgeous women. That's what he knew. That's who he was. Because, hell, what was the alternative? Finding someone special? Making a commitment to someone? Monogamy, for God's sake? He shuddered. Alex didn't *do* commitment. Absolutely not. Not after what had happened in high school.

Alex rolled down the window of his silver Maserati GranTurismo, trying to enjoy the crisp air of the fall evening mingling with the smells of the city. His thoughts invariably turned to his date for tonight, and he wondered, without much excitement and a fair amount of anxiety, if date number three meant he'd be getting into Margaret's thong. On one hand, he was looking for someone—*anyone*—to pull him out of his slump. On the other hand, he wasn't anxious to end the night feeling empty and depressed either.

He cut his engine in front of Margaret's apartment building and checked his reflection in the rearview mirror. The crisp white of his tux shirt was stark against the tan of his neck, and his deep-blue, heavy-lidded, bedroom eyes were fringed with long lashes that women had oohed and aahed over for as long as Alex could remember. He rolled his eyes at his reflection before walking into the apartment building with his head down, wishing he didn't feel so uncertain of himself, wishing he could figure out what would assuage the ache and make him feel like Alex English again.

Heading for the ancient elevator, Alex pressed the call button and turned to look at the opulent lobby of Margaret's building as he waited. Gilded mirrors made the space look even larger and grander as objects multiplied into eternity. Objects like an ornate sconce, a silk brocade love seat, and the delectable curve of a woman's bare back in a black satin evening gown. Delighted by such an appealing distraction, Alex turned around slowly, his eyes sweeping past the sconce and love seat to the woman on the far side of the room. She was tall and slim, and the very simple, sleek lines of her dress showed every curve: her breasts, her waist, her hips, her tight, round ass. The low V of the draped back cutout stopped at the base of her spine, and he followed the line up to her neck, which was swanlike: long and elegant. Her jet-black hair, the same color as the dress, was long enough to be worn over one shoulder, the thick, shiny strands waving uniformly, void of any decoration.

From behind, she was a goddess, and as the elevator rang to announce its arrival, Alex ignored it, staring at the back of the stunning creature that held a black coat over one arm, looking, through the floor-to-ceiling window, at the rain-soaked sidewalk, as though waiting for someone to find her.

"Alex? Alex English?"

Alex whipped his head to the voice coming out of the elevator and was surprised to see his good friend, Cameron Winslow, step toward him wearing a tux and a cheerful smile.

"Hell, I thought that was you!"

"Cam. Good to see you." Alex cleared his throat, darting a quick look at the woman across the lobby, who hadn't turned around, before looking back at his old friend. "What are you doing here?"

Cam took Alex's hand in a hearty shake. "Didn't you know? I moved here. I bought a condo upstairs."

"I had no idea."

Cam grinned, nodding. "Closer to the action, eh, *Professor*?"

"It's a great neighborhood," said Alex, holding back a cringe at his college nickname. "I'm just around the corner."

"The old make-out pad, eh?"

"You know me," said Alex, by rote, knowing the words were expected.

"Yes, I do, and I thank God I wasn't born a woman."

"Not that I'd bang your ugly mug if you were."

"I don't know how you do it."

Lately, I don't. Not like I used to.

He forced a trademark Alex English smirk. "I love the ladies, Cam. Have to keep them happy."

Cam chuckled. "Hey, did you get my message about squash the Thursday after next?"

"After Thanksgiving? No. Are we still on?"

"As long as you're up for an ass whipping. Chris wants to play too, so I suggested doubles. Can you get Fitz or Stratton on board?"

"I'll work on it."

"Great." Cam looked around the lobby for a moment, then, after catching sight of the girl in black by the window, returned his glance to Alex. The change in his face was unmistakable, shifting from congenial to wary on a dime. "Well, I guess I better be going."

Alex raised an eyebrow, flicking his chin toward the goddess. "Is she with you?"

Cam's eyes narrowed just a touch. "In a manner of speaking."

"What manner might that be?" Alex smirked knowingly.

"It's not like that," said Cam sharply, and Alex heard the warning in his friend's voice. Cam's lips tightened to a straight line as he looked at the girl and then back at Alex. "You don't recognize her?"

"I'm looking at her back." Alex shrugged. "Should I?"

"No," grunted Cam, looking increasingly annoyed. "It doesn't matter. Hands off. She's not for you."

"Protective, aren't we, Winslow? Why not let the lady decide?"

"No, Alex. Not *this* lady," said Cam in warning, which surprised Alex, because if she was Cam's girlfriend, Cam should have just said that, but he hadn't.

"What makes this one so special?" asked Alex.

Cam's eyes were icy as he stared at Alex, never dropping his friend's eyes as he called, "Jessica!" in the girl's direction.

Alex looked away from Cam to watch the goddess turn around slowly. If Alex had been rendered almost speechless by the perfection of her back, the wind was knocked out of him as he caught sight of her face.

Her black hair curled down over her shoulder in soft waves, but she pushed it back as she stepped toward Cameron. Her skin was so light and flawless that her bowed, red-painted lips drew his eyes like a beacon, and when she smiled, his heart stopped beating for just a second, as if stunned or disbelieving. He raised his gaze to her eyes and found himself captivated by a green so clear and impossible, it made her eyes sparkle like emeralds behind long, dark lashes. She gazed with warmth at Cameron Winslow, the lucky bastard, as she moved gracefully across the marble floor. Out of respect for his friend's claim on her, Alex was careful not to drop his eyes hungrily to her body, but peripherally, he could see her breasts, high and full, pushed against the thick satin of her dress. The deep plunge in the neckline meant the valley between her breasts was on full, luscious display, and his fingers twitched with longing by his sides, the word *touch, touch, touch,* circling around his head like a magic spell.

His mouth watered as she came closer, bringing with her the scent of tea rose. She cocked her head to the side, and her eyes widened in recognition as she looked at Alex. Something pinged in his memory, but his mind was at sixes and sevens, blown away by her beauty, unable to process that, yes, she did look more than a little familiar to him.

Stopping next to Cameron, she grinned back at Alex merrily.

"Jessica," said Cam tightly, "I don't know if you'll remember—"

"Alex English," she said in a lightly accented voice. "Of course."

No doubt noting the blank expression on his face, she laughed softly. "But I am fairly certain he doesn't remember me."

"I . . . I'm so sorry I don't—"

Alex's brain had ceased working the moment she'd turned around, but he was suddenly struck again by the brilliance of her eyes, and flicking a quick glance to Cameron, he realized the color was almost the same. *Oh my God. She's . . . your . . .*

"By George, I think he's got it!"

"Jessica," murmured Alex. "*Jessie*? Jessie *Winslow*?"

"The very same," she answered, chuckling again.

"The last time I saw you, you were seven years old."

"Nine."

Fourteen years ago.

Without thinking, he dropped his eyes from her face to the creamy skin of her neck, following the graceful line of her throat to her breasts, still lower, down to her waist—

"Alex," warned Cam with genuine menace, making Alex's neck snap back up. "If you don't stop checking out my little sister, God help me, it'll be the last thing you ever do."

"Sorry," said Alex, rubbing his jaw with his thumb and forefinger, trying to compose himself, and desperately trying to reconcile his memories of little Jessie Winslow, who grew up down the street from him, with the heart-stoppingly beautiful, sophisticated creature before him.

Of all the children who'd grown up on Blueberry Lane together, little Jessie had been Alex's unambiguous favorite. Alex had always had a soft spot for her, telling her that "No Girls Allowed" nailed to his clubhouse didn't apply to her and letting her play flashlight tag as his partner when the other older kids told her to get lost. She was six years younger than he, and she'd always been slim and wide-eyed. With her wild tangle of jet-black hair, Alex had found her achingly vulnerable. She'd been special to him—the way she'd look up at him with those big green eyes, trusting him to let her into the clubhouse or let her play with the big kids under his protection, trusting him to be kind to her, trusting him to make the right decision where she was concerned. People looked at Barrett like that all the time, Fitz too, but nobody else had *ever* looked at Alex like that. Ever.

Except Jessie.

"You're all grown up," he said, trying to steady his voice, trying to calm the fierce rushing of his blood as he stared at her. "And you're finally home."

"Just for a visit," cautioned Cam in a low, argumentative voice. "My mother and Jessie are just home for a month, from Thanksgiving to Christmas."

Alex nodded respectfully at Cam before turning back to Jessie. "Staying at Westerly?" he asked, referring to the Winslow estate, just down the road from Alex's childhood home, Haverford Park.

"Where else?" she asked with sparkling eyes.

"I hope we'll see some of you while you're home," said Alex.

"Me too," she said as Cam muttered, "Unlikely" at the same time.

Cam cleared his throat. "Well, Jess and I are on our way out . . ."

"So I gathered," said Alex, flicking his eyes down to the deep V of her neckline approvingly. Her eyes were darker when he caught them again, and heat shot down to his groin with almost uncomfortable precision.

Jessie let her eyes drop for a moment too, lingering on Alex's white tuxedo shirt, before raising them. "You're headed somewhere too?"

"Yes." He shook his head briefly as his schedule for the evening reasserted itself. If spending his evening with Margaret Story had seemed a drab plan fifteen minutes ago, now it felt positively unbearable. He gestured limply to the elevator. "We, um, we're headed to the Union League Club."

"What a coincidence," said Jessie. "That's where we're going. I guess we'll see you there?"

At Alex's mention of *we,* her eyes had lost a hint of their luster, and it surprised Alex how much he wanted to restore it, but before he could say anything—

"*We*?" asked Cam, looking relieved for the first time since calling Jessie over. "Who's your date?"

"Margaret Story."

"Margaret. Wonderful girl. Haven't seen the Story sisters in ages," said Cam, referring to the family of five sisters who had also grown up on Blueberry Lane, in Forrester, the mansion across the street from the Winslows' Westerly. "I didn't realize you two were together."

Alex flinched. In no way did he want for Jessie to believe that he was seriously dating someone. He started stumbling over his words to explain. "It's not like that. We're just—"

"We don't need the sordid details, *Professor*."

Alex stiffened. Generally he rolled his eyes or smirked at the nickname, but he hated the way it sounded in front of Jessie. "No. It's not like that. We're not a couple. I mean, Margaret and I aren't—"

"Aren't what?"

Alex whipped his head around to find Margaret Story standing behind him, her chestnut brown hair in a smart chignon, wearing a Grecian-style, gold lamé gown. She looked elegant and sophisticated, but she couldn't hold a candle to the fresh, young beauty of Jessica Winslow. His whole body deflated at the sight of Margaret, and the familiar ache, which he hadn't noticed as he chatted with Cam and Jessie, returned.

"Margaret," Alex said, rubbing his chest and giving her an apologetic smile.

"Hello, Margaret," said Cam, leaning forward to kiss her cheek. "You look smashing."

"Hello, Cam. I heard through the grapevine that we're neighbors now?"

"That's right. Come by for sugar anytime."

Margaret chuckled politely, but her shrewd gaze flicked to Jessica, almost ten years her junior. Alex watched as Margaret put together the pieces of the conversation she'd walked in on. "Jessie Winslow, I'd know you anywhere, though I can't remember the last time I saw you."

"It's been years." Jessica held out her hand and smiled warmly at Margaret. "How is your sister Jane?"

"Very well," said Margaret, her shoulders relaxing just a little. "I'll be sure to say hello for you."

"Please do. I'd love to see her while I'm visiting."

"Visiting." Margaret glanced at Alex, who nodded to confirm this bit of information, then back at Jessie.

"I'm just here for the holidays," clarified Jessie, handing her coat to Cameron, who held it for her.

Alex had never felt jealous of a coat before, but as she pulled the lapels close to her throat and tied the satin sash around her tiny waist, he wished he could hold her so closely, feel those curves pressed so intimately against him.

If it discomposed Jessie to lift her eyes and find Alex gaping hungrily at her, she didn't let it show. Her eyes softened as they searched his, and her lips tilted up in a sweet, sad smile.

"It was good to see you," she murmured before Cam took her arm and ushered her out the door to a waiting cab. Alex watched as the doorman closed the door behind her, as she stepped into the cab, as the taillights sped away.

"Ahem," said Margaret from beside him, and he turned to look at her.

"Margaret, I'm—"

"If you were me, what would you do?"

"I'm so sorry," he said, taking the black velvet wrap she held over her arm and holding it for her as she stepped into it. "What do you mean?"

"I *had* intended to invite you up tonight," she said meaningfully, looking down as she tied bows out of the satin ribbons that held the cape closed. "But apparently you and I aren't . . ."

She looked up, raising her eyebrows at him, silently asking him to finish the statement he'd been making as she walked in on their conversation.

"Aren't going to happen," he said softly, surprised as the words left his mouth.

"I see." Margaret nodded once, handling her disappointment with grace. "It probably doesn't make much sense to go to the gala together then."

"I'd still be honored to be your attendant, Margaret," said Alex quickly. "And you won't be lonely. That dress is—as Cam observed—smashing. They'll be lining up in droves."

"Do you think so?"

"I do." Alex nodded, leaning down to kiss her cheek. "You're terrific, Margaret."

"Terrific. Hmm. You know, it doesn't feel so terrific when the—forgive me, Alex, but let's just be honest here—manwhore of the country club turns you down when you're a sure thing."

He stared at Margaret, dumbstruck. Hearing her call him out in such blatant and unflattering terms, no matter their validity, was embarrassing. He felt the heat rush into his cheeks, but on the heels of his shame was an even more alarming thought:

She was right.

There is *something wrong with Alex English,* he thought again, grimacing at her. Not only was his chest aching again, but he was suddenly turning down a sure thing, when he *never* turned down a sure thing. Why? Why would he do that?

It was a really uncomfortable question that Alex wasn't remotely interested in answering.

"I didn't turn you down," he finally pointed out, trying to grin at her, but feeling none of the easiness he normally did when flirting with a woman. "You withdrew the offer."

"I guess." She took a deep breath and nodded. "You know, I haven't gone stag to one of these things in a million years, but I think I'm better off going on my own tonight. No hard feelings?"

"None at all. Sure you don't want to share a cab?"

She shook her head and reached up to place a light kiss on his cheek. "We weren't meant to be, you and me," she said, turning toward the front door of her building as Alex accompanied her to the curb. "But one day I'll say I was there to witness it: the moment the elusive heart of Alex English got sideswiped by a kid."

Chapter 2

Jessie sat beside Cameron in the car to the Union League Club trying to catch her breath and compose herself without looking like anything was amiss. She stared out the window as the streets of Philadelphia zoomed by, trying to focus on something—*anything*—other than Alex English, and was amazed to find that although she'd been away for years, she still recognized landmarks and places. Though London would always be her home, she was pleased to discover that Philly still felt familiar.

After a few minutes, her heart finally stopped pounding, but she was still flustered by her chance encounter with Alex. Seeing him again felt like an almost astonishing twist of fate—of all the friends and family she'd left behind in Philadelphia so long ago, Alex English was the one person she'd desperately hoped to see during her holiday visit. Even though her brain knew that running into him on her first night back was just a coincidence, her heart insisted it was providence.

There hadn't been a moment—not a single moment in the last fourteen years—that Jessie had forgotten him, despite the distance and age difference between them. Alex lived legendary and large in her mind: the fantastically gorgeous boy who lived next door, who'd been so kind to her after her father's death. To her brothers, who had grieved in their own quiet ways, she'd been a nuisance. But not to Alex, who had paid attention to her, included her, and made her feel special. His blue eyes, crinkled and laughing, had accompanied her through every subsequent life transition with the reminder that kindness could exist in unlikely places.

And then there was this . . . adult Alex was scorching hot, oozing a naughty, flirty sex appeal that made her toes curl inside her Manolo heels. If Alex had been a really, really good-looking teenager, he'd grown into a model-beautiful adult. Over six feet tall, with golden blond hair and aqua blue eyes. No movie star on the big screen was sexier than Alex English. He was every woman's wettest, hottest dream, and the bold way he'd raked his eyes down her body made Jessie's insides clench with longing . . .

. . . and reminded her of Alex's reputation. Jessie was young, but she wasn't naïve. She had learned—via Facebook and the Internet—that he was a terrible womanizer and heartbreaker. Inconvenient because, although the rumors would suggest she stay away from him, after catching a glimpse of Alex, her heart longed for more.

"Stay away from him," Cam intoned softly from beside her. Seven years older than Jessie, he had always been protective.

"Don't be ridiculous," said Jessie, looking at her brother. "He's an old family friend."

"Anyone but Alex," said Cam, turning to her, his eyes dark and serious.

Jessie knew that coming back to the United States to visit her four considerably older brothers meant she was going to have to put up with a certain level of watchdogging. Still, she was surprised by how much it rankled. While living in her mother's native London without her brothers, who had returned to the United States to finish college and chosen to make their homes in Philadelphia, Jessie had been free to make her own decisions without their daily influence. She was a twenty-three-year-old woman who had lived abroad for the past fourteen years, chosen boyfriends, enjoyed lovers, and made her own decisions. She didn't require or appreciate Cam's overprotectiveness.

That said, Jessie adored her brothers with the wide-eyed adoration of a much younger sister, and was always anxious to please them. So, instead of arguing with Cam, Jessie changed the subject. "Philly hasn't changed."

"Hey," said Cam, thoughtfully, switching gears. "Were you close to Jane Story?"

"Not terribly, though I'd say we were friendly. The Storys were members at Silver Springs just like we were, so I saw Jane at the club every summer for swim team and tennis team. I liked her."

"Margaret sure looked different."

Jessie grinned to herself, looking out the window. Margaret Story, with her petite build and dark brown hair, was exactly Cameron's type. And how convenient that she lived in the same building now.

"I wonder why she's slumming with Alex English?" he mused aloud.

Jessie bristled in Alex's defense, but kept a tart rejoinder to herself. Cam was hardly an angel with the ladies. While he didn't rival Alex's reputation, he was no choirboy either.

"It didn't look serious to me. I'm sure they're just friends."

"Alex doesn't *do* friends," said Cam, his brows creasing. "Not with women. Doesn't have girlfriends either. He doesn't do commitment, Jess. Never has, never will."

"Margaret will be here tonight," said Jessie gently, ignoring Cam's meaning as she gestured to the austere granite-and-brick building she recognized as the Union League Club. "Ask her to dance. You'll be able to figure out if there's anything serious going on between her and Alex."

He turned to her as the car pulled up to the curb. "Just remember what I said about him."

"At some point, you're going to have to notice that I can take care of myself."

Cameron rolled his eyes, then paid the driver and got out to open her door. As Jessie stepped under the awning and into the Union League Club, she thought about Cam's warning. *Alex doesn't* do *friends.* Thinking about what Alex *did* do made her heart skip a beat as Cam ushered her toward the small dining room where they'd have supper before the gala.

Even though Cam's Neanderthal warning grated on her sense of independence, he was probably right. Despite the way her heart had surged to be reunited with him, Alex was a notorious scoundrel, and according to most reports, a short fling was the most any woman could expect from him. Not one for flings, it would be best for Jessie to stay out of his way.

She sat on the chair Cam held for her, searching his eyes, which still glowered with a warning. Her spirits plunged at the thought of avoiding Alex during her visit, even though it might be for the best . . .

. . . unless Cam was wrong.

Cam said that Alex didn't "do" friends, but that wasn't entirely true. She and Alex had been childhood friends once upon a time, and he was still a good friend to her brother. She thought of the boy who'd been so kind to her when she was young, and her lips turned up with hope. Surely someone from his childhood, whom he'd known forever, could be the exception to the Alex-doesn't-do-friends rule.

Surely we can be friends, she thought, smiling at Cam and wondering if it was possible to reconnect with Alex English without riling her brothers *or* risking the safety of her heart.

After taking a cab to the club on his own, Alex found himself leaning against the edge of the bar, searching the room unsuccessfully for Jessie Winslow. She and Cam must have decided to have dinner first, which was good since it gave him a bit of time to think.

Margaret's parting words had been bothering Alex, especially since he couldn't argue with them. He actually felt sideswiped. His whole body felt electric after running into a girl he hadn't seen since she was in pigtails. And while part of Alex was grateful to feel *something,* other than the gaping ache that seemed to have subsided for tonight, a larger part of him was wary of the depth and strength of his reaction to Jessie. Alex had always been an equal opportunity womanizer—so focusing all his attention on one woman, even for an hour at a gala, felt wildly unfamiliar. But hell if he could even look at another woman since seeing Jessie. The ballroom was filled with stunning women who were trying unsuccessfully to catch his eye. He barely noted them.

Taking another long swig of scotch, he placed his empty glass back on the corner of the bar, winking at the bartender to ask for a refill. Despite the two long lines of party guests waiting their turns to order a drink, she stopped shaking mid-martini to refill his glass.

"I get off at ten," she said, wetting her lips as she replaced the cocktail napkin under his fresh drink. It had her phone number written on it with the name Traci, the *i* dotted with a tiny heart.

"Is that right?"

"Mm-hm."

"Tempting," he lied, because words like that rolled off his tongue without much thought.

"I'll look for you at 9:59," she said, biting her lower lip before sauntering away.

And though Alex had no intention of swinging back at ten, he still checked out her ass as she turned to help the next person in line. *Not bad.*

Alex wasn't at all surprised by the bartender's come-on. While Barrett had always attracted the sort of respectable attention befitting the fair-haired firstborn of their family, from his early teens Alex's smoldering good looks and natural physique had attracted a different sort of attention altogether. Winks and licked lips, thrusted breasts and lowered lashes.

With lips, breasts, and lashes on his mind, his thoughts segued easily back to Jessie. She was all grown up now. She'd been living in England for years, but the Internet made the world very small. He wondered how much she knew about his reputation. For the most part, Alex didn't give a damn what people thought or said about him—half of it wasn't even true, just part of the myth surrounding him—but for the first time in a long time, he wished he'd lived his life a little more respectably, a little more like Barrett.

"Bor-ing."

Deep in thought, Alex didn't notice his youngest brother, Weston, sidle up, leaning against the bar beside him.

"It's a fund-raiser. What were you expecting, Romper Room?"

"Do not call me that or I will deck you."

"You and who else?"

Weston looked out over the grand ballroom of the club, over the heads of the couples dancing and the elaborate dessert buffet, sighting their older brothers, Barrett and Fitz. They stood across the room with their fiancées, Emily and Daisy, talking to an older couple.

"Fitz'll do it. He loves whaling on you."

"Fitz is losing his edge as we speak," said Alex derisively. "I think I see his balls jutting out of Daisy's purse. Uh . . . yep. There they are."

As Alex stared at his brothers, the ache asserted itself, making Alex's chest tighten and forcing him to look away as he took a generous gulp of scotch. While Alex didn't have anything against marriage per se, it was hard for him to understand why any man would want to tie himself to one woman when there was a world full of gorgeous women to enjoy.

That thought concluded, and he avoided eye contact with about a dozen gorgeous women as he unsuccessfully scanned the room for Jessica Winslow again. When his eyes landed back on Fitz, who was gazing at Daisy with something stomach-churningly close to adoration, Alex grimaced, turning back to Weston.

"Fine," said Wes. "I'll get Stratton to do it, then."

Alex straightened a little. "Is he even here? He hates these things."

"Yeah. He's not staying long, but he showed up for Mom."

"I'll give it to Strat. He's buff. He could take me." He looked over the crowd of heads for Stratton's wavy, blond hair. "Where is he?"

"Where's who?" asked Stratton, flanking Alex's other side out of nowhere.

"You. Romper Room here said you'd kick my ass if I cast any further aspersions on his character."

"What're you paying these days, Wes?" asked Stratton, sipping on something bright green that looked like antifreeze.

"What the hell are you drinking?" asked Alex, shaking his head at the girly drink. "All you're missing is a hot-pink umbrella in that thing."

"Midori Sour," he answered.

"Are *your* balls in Daisy's purse too?" asked Alex.

"Fifty bucks," interjected Weston. "A hundred if you make him bleed."

"Wait a sec," said Stratton. "I think he's insulting *me* now. I might do it for free. Call Wes Romper Room again, Alex."

"Screw you, Strat. Get in line and order a real man's drink."

"*Jesus*," hissed Wes in amazement, which silenced his squabbling brothers. "Who the hell is *that*?"

Alex followed his younger brother's eyes to see Jessica walking into the ballroom beside Cameron. Quickly clocking the dozen or so hungry eyes around the room sharing Weston's admiration, he realized Wes wasn't the only man who'd noticed the most beautiful girl in the universe had just walked into the ballroom of the Union League Club.

"It's Jessica Winslow," said Stratton matter-of-factly, and Alex could have kissed him for looking away from her like he was immune to her stunning beauty. *One down, a million to go.*

Weston elbowed Alex in the side. "Someone's all grown up, huh? Wow. Where do I get in line?"

"Shut up, Wes," said Alex in a low, irritated voice.

"What's *your* problem?" asked Weston. "I'd think you'd be the first up to hit that."

"Seriously, shut your mouth. She's an old family friend. Show some respect."

"*Respect*?" Weston's mouth dropped open. "What the hell? Did you have a brain transplant this afternoon?"

"Don't be an asshole. She's a nice girl."

"So's Hope Atwell, but everyone knows about your Thursday nooners at the Four Seasons with her."

This was actually news to Alex. He didn't realize his standing date with Hope was common knowledge among his peers, and while Alex didn't exactly live his life with much modesty or privacy, he found himself feeling strangely annoyed.

"Hope's not *that* nice," said Alex, his back flexing from where her fingernails had broken the skin on Thursday afternoon.

"It's bad enough that Barrett threw over her sister Felicity. Now you're treating Hope like a common slut. The Atwell girls have every right to hate us."

"Neither of us took anything they didn't offer."

Alex tracked Jessie as she shook hands with some friends of Cam's, and his fingers fisted as he watched J.C. Rousseau look down at her breasts, then widen his smile.

Meanwhile, Wes was acting like a dog with a bone. "I'm just saying, you don't have a lot of room to be defending nice girls, Alex. You're my brother, but you're an asshole to women, and everyone here knows it."

That got Alex's back up. English brothers might give each other a hard time now and then, but loyalty was still the code they adhered to among each other, and Weston's words sounded suspiciously disloyal in Alex's ears. His eyes cut to Weston's, but before he could take a swing to teach the brat a lesson, Stratton stepped forward, placing his body between his brothers. "Enough, Wes."

"Screw you, Strat. You don't know. You don't—" Weston cringed, shaking his head, then turned on his heel and walked away angrily, disappearing into the crowd.

"What the *hell* was that all about?"

"Christ, you're thick," said Stratton, finishing his drink and shaking his head no when the bartender caught his eyes quickly to see if he wanted another. "He's been in love with Constance Atwell since the beginning of time."

"Shoot," said Alex. "I didn't know."

"Obviously. But between you and Barrett, you've probably screwed his chances with her."

"I'll break things off with Hope."

"Yeah," deadpanned Stratton. "Dump her. That'll help."

"Damn it." Alex sighed. He'd need to figure out how to let Hope down easy so he didn't ruin things further for Wes. He shook his head before searching for Jessie in the crowd. And when he found her, his heart dropped just a little, scattering his thoughts, only one breaking through the surface to forcefully assert itself through his haze of lust and longing.

"God, she's beautiful, isn't she?"

Stratton glanced at her and shrugged. "I don't know her."

Alex's eyes cut to his younger brother. "What the hell does that have to do with how beautiful she is?"

Stratton flinched and shook his head. "Nothing. I think I'll head home. See you Sunday?"

"Sure," answered Alex, running a hand through his hair as he watched Stratton stalk away and hating that he now felt at odds with two brothers.

He'd inadvertently hurt Weston, and he wished he understood Stratton better.

Stratton was arguably the best looking of the English brothers—he was the tallest, the most ripped. Hell, add to that, he was the only English brother with dimples like craters. Lots of women checked out Strat, but Strat seemed to see only the ones who *didn't* check out him.

Alex had seen it dozens of times: Stratton would spend a party talking to some girl in the stairwell about how much she missed her ex-boyfriend. She'd cry all over him, he'd listen sympathetically, and at the end of the night, he'd put her in a cab as she waved good-bye and called him a "total sweetie." And Stratton didn't even seem especially bothered. He'd ignore all the other women drooling over him, catch another cab for himself, go home, open up his Kindle, and spend his evening quietly alone, oblivious to the wide world of pussy that was his for the taking.

Alex didn't get it. Never had. Never would.

He watched as Stratton made his way through the crowd, pausing to stop and talk to someone for a moment. Only after Stratton continued moving forward, toward the exit, did the crowd clear, and Alex realized it was Jessie.

She grinned at him as she made her way to the bar. She hadn't seen Alex when she first entered the ballroom, but she'd seen Weston, then Stratton, come from the direction of the bar, and hedged her bets that where there were two English brothers, there might be a third. She was glad she'd been right.

Alex straightened up as she approached, a smile widening across his face as he held her eyes with his.

"Hi again," she said, a way-more-than-just-friends happiness making her belly flutter to be near him again so soon.

"Hi," he said, staring at her. He laughed softly, shaking his head with a look of amused amazement as he raised his glass for a sip. "That was some entrance."

"Oh, yeah?"

"Mmm. You got the attention of every Y chromosome in the room."

"Including yours?"

"You've had mine for"—Alex twisted his wrist and looked at his watch—"about seventeen years."

Jessie had expected him to say *an hour*, but she was delighted by his reference to their shared childhood and chuckled lightly before looking around for his date.

"Where's Margaret?"

"She decided she was better off attending stag tonight."

The fluttering in Jessie's tummy doubled, but she kept her face placid, tilting her head to the side. "Am I sorry to hear that?"

"Nope. You're not." His full, delicious lips curved into a grin, and he shrugged, which only made him more adorable.

Her cheeks warmed from his teasing grin. "So what are we drinking?"

"Scotch. But the last time I saw you, you were nine. I feel like you should be drinking milk. Or a juice box."

"And yet your eyes seem to have realized that I'm all grown up."

It was much too bold an observation for one friend to make to another, but the way he looked at her was making all thoughts of friendship fly out the window. Jessie deliberately took a deep breath so that her breasts would swell and hold against the already-daring neckline of her dress. Alex dropped his eyes to her cleavage, and she heard his sharp intake of breath before he dragged his eyes back up to her face. He clenched his jaw, his eyes dark and laser-focused on hers.

"It would be impossible to miss."

Her skin tingled with awareness, and she finally exhaled, dropping his gaze, only to notice Cameron making his way around the ballroom. The delightful rush she felt from talking to Alex slipped away, and she tensed immediately. Her brother hadn't spotted her yet, but if he saw her talking to Alex, it was entirely possible he'd make a scene.

She cut her eyes to Alex, offering him a nervous grin. "It's so warm in here. Grab me a martini and meet me on the balcony?"

"How do you want it?" he asked.

Biting her bottom lip, she leaned toward him, placing her hand on his arm and whispering low in his ear, "Dirty."

She caught the brief widening of his eyes as she drew back, but before he could say anything else, she turned, weaving through the crowd until she reached the French doors that led outside to an intimate balcony. She was greeted by a blast of chilly air, like a smack in the face, reminding her that she was supposed to be forging a path to friendship, not acting like a first-class flirt.

"Dirty?" she demanded aloud. "Really, Jess?"

Her cheeks were still flushed from her exchange with Alex, and she pressed her palms against them as she stepped up to the cement balustrade that looked out over Broad Street. When she'd exchanged hellos with his brother, she peeked around Stratton to check him out, debonair and bored, leaning up against the bar. But the instant he saw her, his body language changed completely. The awed expression on his face was like a shot to her heart, and he straightened, lowering his glass to his side. But it was his eyes that had so affected her—they were openly and nakedly delighted, wide with admiration. There was no smarmy artifice in his gaze, only the sort of happiness that spreads across the face of someone genuinely enchanted. Jessie sensed that it wasn't a typical smile for Alex. As soon as he raised his glass and took a sip, he slipped back into his Alex English persona.

What would it be like, she wondered, if the two parts of Alex could be reversed—if the genuine, openhearted man she'd glimpsed for a moment could gradually overcome the player? Was it even possible?

Hearing the click of the door opening, she turned around to face him, resting her hands on the cold concrete behind her.

"A dirty martini for mademoiselle?" he said, holding out an elegant, frosted glass with cloudy liquid as he pushed the door closed with his foot.

She stepped forward, accepting the glass and touching it lightly to his.

"You drink scotch," she said, determined to stop flirting and offer some friendly conversation.

"Mm-hm."

"What's your favorite kind? I've been dragged all over Scotland by school chums. I'm a veritable expert."

"Is that right?"

"Mmm," she said, taking a sip of her drink before putting it gently on the wide concrete surface behind her. "Try me."

"Speyside single malt," he said, raising his eyebrows in challenge.

"Very specific," she answered. Speyside, an area of northeastern Scotland located around the Spey River valley, was home to over thirty different distilleries, almost all of which Jessie had visited more than once. She couldn't help trying to impress him. "I'm guessing Glenfiddich? Or Macallan?"

His grin was a mix of surprise and admiration. "Aberlour fifteen year, when I can get it."

She lowered her lashes, looking at his glass incredulously. "They have Aberlour here?"

Alex nodded, and Jessie understood. They kept a bottle on hand for him.

"The perks of being an English," she said lightly.

"This from a Winslow," he teased.

He held her eyes, and the shiver that made her tremble had nothing to do with the chilly November weather.

The entire space of the balcony wasn't more than the size of a double closet, but he stepped closer to her, setting his drink beside hers and shrugging out of his jacket. Without asking permission, he circled it around her shoulders, pulling the lapels together at the base of her throat until his knuckles touched, the backs of his fingers brushing against her skin.

Jessie's breath caught as she looked up at him. All he'd have to do is drop his head and his lips would touch hers. And though they'd been reacquainted for only a handful of minutes, and though she knew that if he kissed her, any chance of rekindling a childhood friendship would be tossed out the window, there was nothing she wanted more in that moment than for Alex to kiss her.

"You shouldn't be out here with me," he said softly, searching her eyes and frowning.

"Why not?"

"Your brother would kill you. And me. Me first."

He still hadn't moved his hands from where they rested against her skin. Jessie took a step toward him, still looking into his eyes.

"I'm an adult. My brothers aren't in charge of me."

He drew his hands away, stepping back until he leaned against one of the two French doors that led back into the ballroom.

"Jess. You haven't lived here for a long time. You don't know who I am. You don't know what people think of me, what they say about me."

"We have Facebook in London, Alex," she said, pushing her arms through his warm jacket before reaching for her glass again.

"Oh." He winced. "So you know. You already know who I am."

"I know who you are. You held my hand and let me be your partner for flashlight tag when I was six and so lonesome for my father I thought I'd go crazy from it. You're the person who told me that 'No Girls Allowed' didn't apply to me when I was seven. You gave me my first kiss, on the forehead, when I was nine and my mother announced we were moving to England to be closer to her family. You're Alex English, the person who was kind to me when I was scared, when I was left out, when my heart was breaking." Her voice was thready with emotion, so she stopped speaking for a moment, offering him the bravest smile she could manage before finishing her little speech. "I know exactly who you are."

Chapter 3

Alex's heart, which had been unaffected by any woman for more years than he could count, was so gripped in the vise of Jessie's words, he realized at some point that he was speechless. His drink held suspended in his hand, his breath trapped in his chest, his eyes glued to hers. It was possible that the world had stopped spinning, because he was fairly certain they were the only two people who existed.

Finally, the burning in his lungs forced him to breathe, and his eyes reverted to familiar, comfortable behavior, dropping hers and checking out her body. He had never been more powerfully attracted to someone. Never. Not after years of conquests and trysts. Jessica was like an instant drug to him, a hit of sweet Ecstasy that was addling his senses. He had a sudden mental image of her in bed beneath him, and he trembled, forcing himself not to reach for her as he dragged his eyes back up to meet hers.

Could she see it? Could she see what he was thinking? He imagined her naked and wanting, arching her back to meet his thrusts, moaning as he stretched her, crying out as she came, her muscles shuddering rhythmically around him.

"Oh," she said, blinking up at him in realization.

Her voice wasn't breathless or shocked, though he noticed her breasts heaved against her dress just a little bit harder than they had a moment before. That slight, but unmistakable, shift in her breathing would almost be enough for a man looking for an opening to make a move on her.

But instead of taking a step forward to pull her against him—to see if he was right and if kissing her perfect lips would lead to a passionate, impromptu fuck against the brick wall of a cold, dark balcony—Alex froze. The same eyes that had trusted him as a child now looked at him as an adult, and he was powerless to misuse her. Every protective instinct rose within him, and all he could think was that he needed to stay away from her.

"We'll go back inside separately," he said softly, exhaling in a rush as his body, primed and ready for pleasure, balked that none was forthcoming. "You go first. I'll wait a while, and then—"

"Alex, your reputation doesn't bother me. Didn't you hear what I said?" she asked, her forehead deeply creased in confusion.

"Yes. Every word," Alex said through clenched teeth. He winced, shaking his head. There was something wrong with him—something *deeply wrong* with him—if he didn't at least reach for this living goddess. "But I'm no good for you, Jess."

"I see," she said softly, pulling his jacket more snugly over her chest, which released a strong whiff of Polo Black. He fleetingly wondered if she would smell like him when she took it off. Glancing back at her face, it surprised him when her stunning red lips tilted up in a sweet, understanding smile. "But I didn't actually offer anything, Alex."

"Didn't you?" he asked, fairly certain he'd seen the offer in her eyes, even if she wasn't aware she'd made it.

She shook her head. "I just wanted you to know that I don't judge you for your personal choices. You were a friend to me when I needed one. And though I'm sure you don't need one, I'd like to be yours all the same."

Her words were like a bucket of cold water over his head, and Alex didn't know whether to be touched or slighted.

Friendship? She was offering him *friendship*? Was she actually saying she didn't want to date him or sleep with him or otherwise learn what it would feel like to be with Alex English? He searched her face, but it was pristine and unstudied in the moonlight, her eyes earnest, if a little sad. She wanted to be his . . . *friend*? Alex didn't know how to be friends with a woman. The few times he'd tried, he'd ended up sleeping with them anyway.

"Friends," he said, trying not to grimace.

She nodded, smiling brightly at him like their being friends was an actual possibility when his body was raging with want for her.

"Or do you not do friends?"

"Oh, I definitely *do* friends," said Alex without thinking.

He grimaced in embarrassment, but to his relief, Jessie wasn't at all offended. Her eyes widened, and her mouth dropped open softly before she started laughing. It was musical and soft, a sound so welcome Alex found himself grinning and wishing he could hear Jessie Winslow laugh every day for the rest of his life.

Finally she took another sip of her martini, shaking her head, her face a mixture of amusement and skepticism. "Do lines like that actually work?"

"You'd be surprised."

"I guess I would be." She tilted her head to the side and grinned. "What's your best one?"

"Really?"

"Yeah. Lay it on me."

He studied her face, but it was open and amused, and he decided to answer her honestly.

"Are you an interior decorator?"

"No," she said, looking confused by the sudden shift in conversation.

"Because the whole room got more beautiful when you walked into it."

She gasped before breaking into gales of laughter, her shoulders shaking under his oversize jacket. When she could finally speak, she demanded, "Tell me another."

He gave her one of his sexier smiles, then dropped his eyes obviously to her chest. When she smacked his arm, he looked up, wide-eyed and startled.

"I wasn't staring at your breasts," he insisted. "I was staring at your heart."

"Oh. My. God," she chortled, setting down her drink with shaky hands as she wheezed softly from laughing.

"Want another?" he asked eagerly, wanting to hear her laugh again.

"Tell me the cheesiest of the cheesy."

Alex nodded. "Okay." He cleared his face of all expression, softened his lips, and looked deeply into her eyes. "Of all the beautiful curves on your body . . . your smile is my favorite."

He watched closely, waiting for her to burst into laughter again, but she blushed and took a deep breath instead, an uncertain smile playing at the edges of her mouth. "You're good."

"Actually," he said, taking a step closer to her, "I'm very bad."

"Oh Lord!" she exclaimed, pushing his chest away and giggling all over again. "That one was the worst!"

He took a step back, snapping his fingers dramatically. "Overplayed my hand. Almost thought I had you there on the smile line."

"Maybe you almost did." She gave him a bashful grin before reaching for her glass and taking a sip.

"They don't work for you?" he asked. "Pickup lines?"

"They're kind of silly, aren't they?"

"Some women think they're sexy."

She shrugged, her wide eyes merry as she continued to grin.

"Okay. You win. They're silly. So what *does* work for you?" he asked, unable to resist learning a little more about her, surprised to discover, for the first time in years, he actually *wanted* to hear a woman talk about herself.

Her smile faded a bit, and if the light had been stronger, he was sure he'd notice a self-conscious blush deepen the pink on her cheeks. "Really?"

"Yeah. I want to know."

"I don't know if it's very *sexy*," she said, referring to his previous comment.

"Tell me anyway."

"Huh. Okay. Here goes. What works for me? Kindness. Respect. Someone who makes me laugh." She grinned more confidently at him, and her shoulders relaxed as she eased into the subject. "Someone smart and interesting. A little daring maybe. Someone who surprises me in good ways."

"What else?"

"Someone who makes my toes curl when he kisses me."

"What else?" he whispered.

"Someone who lets me put my cold feet against his warm legs."

"More," he said softly, mesmerized by her simple honesty.

She shook her head, searching his face, before taking another sip of her drink. "Someone who can't take his eyes off me."

Her eyes were pools of black staring back at his, and he could feel the heat, the longing, the charged field of want between them.

"What else?" His voice was barely audible as he breathed heavily, in and out, in and out, through his nose, the warmth of his breath making puffs of smoke every time he exhaled.

She swallowed, still holding his eyes.

"Someone who chooses me," she whispered, her smile all but faded. "*Only* me."

Alex raised his chin just a touch, searching her eyes. He understood what she was saying. She wasn't the sort of woman who'd fall for his lines or end up on her back in his bed tonight. She was a nice girl looking for a nice boy, and Alex was the furthest possible thing from the solid, committed, upstanding man Jessie deserved.

What surprised him was how much it *ached* to hear it—to realize that he couldn't have her, that, as he was, he wasn't good enough for her. At that moment, he knew how much he wanted to indulge the fantasy of having a chance with her. His disappointment was far more bitter and painful than he would have guessed.

He nodded curtly, giving her a tight smile, and turned to leave. Her voice at his back made him pause.

"Dance with me?" she murmured suddenly, looking as surprised as he felt to hear the words tumble from her mouth. She dropped his eyes, flicking her glance to the French doors behind him as the orchestra started playing the old ballroom standard "The Way You Look Tonight." "This is one of my favorites."

"It's not a good idea, Jess," he said, her words "only me" fresh in his head. He thought of Cameron's warning, about the little girl who trusted him once upon a time. He reminded himself that he was not the sort of man who deserved someone like her, on any level.

"I don't care." Her eyes flashed, meeting his with intensity before softening with a small, cajoling smile. "Don't friends ever dance together?"

"I'm the wrong person to ask. When I'm dancing with someone, I'm generally trying to get into her pants."

"Oh," said Jessie, pushing away from the low cement wall to stand before him. "Then it's okay, because I'm wearing a dress."

She drew his hand to her hip, under his jacket, placing his palm flat against the smooth satin, and he pulled her toward him as his fingers spread, then tightened. She bent her head back to look up at him, her lips catching the ambient light from the ballroom, shiny and full, heart-wrenchingly lovely. She placed one hand on his shoulder and held up the other, waiting for him to take it in his. Knowing what a very bad idea it was to slow-dance with Jessica Winslow on the secluded balcony, he still couldn't help himself from reaching for her, from stealing this one fleeting moment before telling her good-bye.

She gasped lightly as his fingers curled around her hand, and he cut his eyes from their joined hands to her face. Her tongue slipped between her lips to wet them, and Alex watched, fascinated, his chest heaving from the feeling of holding her so close.

With dance steps well practiced at Simon West's School of Dance, they made the best of the small space, their movements tight. Alex tried not to look at her face, which was so beautiful and unguarded he could barely stand not to lean down and kiss her. He lifted his chin and stared, instead, over her shoulder at the lights of the cars moving back and forth on the street below. A dozen cars going somewhere. A dozen people who had no idea how much the world had changed in the past hour.

Jessica Winslow was home after fourteen years. She was stunning and witty and warm, and she wanted to be friends. Friends.

Hmm, Alex thought. *She hadn't withdrawn that offer.*

He pulled her closer, feeling desperate to assuage the heaviness he'd feel when the song ended and she walked away from him. No one had ever looked at him as Jessie did, and now that she'd reappeared in his life, even for a handful of weeks, he couldn't bear to let her go. She had offered him her friendship, and Alex was helpless to refuse it.

He looked at the stars, silently promising that he wouldn't make a move on her—he couldn't, *wouldn't*, let himself have her, wouldn't let himself *ruin* her by letting anyone think she was one of the Professor's Girls. He would be careful and discreet, as proper as a parson, if that's what it took to know her again.

"Jess," he whispered close to her ear. He felt her tremble lightly in his arms. "If the offer's still open, I'd like to be friends."

She leaned back, her lips tilting up softly as she searched his eyes. After a long pause, she finally answered, "It's still open."

"Okay, then." He gulped softly, surprised by the leaping in his chest, the sudden lightness of his head. "Friends."

"Friends," she said, giving him an encouraging smile before leaning forward to rest her cheek on his shoulder.

"Um. What does that look like, exactly?" he asked against her hair, closing his eyes, inhaling the light scent of tea roses mixed with Black and knowing that he'd buy another tux before he'd launder the jacket she was wearing tonight.

"It could look like lunch . . . on Tuesday, if you're free. I know it's Thanksgiving week, but—"

"I'm free," he answered. "We'll be discreet."

"Alex, it wouldn't bother me to be seen with you."

Those eyes again. Those trusting eyes that looked into his face like she had some secret knowledge of his heart, like she had some guarantee that he wouldn't hurt her.

Well, she was right. He wouldn't.

He thought about Weston stalking away because his weekly nooners with Hope had ruined Wes's chances with Constance. He thought of Cameron's hard eyes as he warned Alex away from his sister. He couldn't bear for Jessie to be the topic of rumors and speculation—for their mutual acquaintances and her brothers to assume she was just another conquest.

"It would bother *me*. We'll be discreet, or we can't be friends."

She leaned back, a small smile playing at the corners of her mouth. "Okay."

"Shall I have a car pick you up at Cam's or at Westerly on Tuesday?"

"Westerly. I'm just in the city for tonight."

The music faded gently, and Alex heard his mother's voice over the microphone, asking for people to take their seats before her presentation. She was about to make a speech about Save the Children of Philadelphia, and it was the perfect time for Alex to slip back inside unnoticed.

He let go of Jessie regretfully, and she shrugged out of his jacket, holding it out to him. He put it back on quickly, savoring the warmth from her body, the faint smell of her perfume. Just before he turned away from her, he couldn't resist taking her hand and raising it to his lips, resting them against the soft warmth of her skin for a single moment before slipping back inside.

Jessie put her hand to her chest after he was gone. Her heart thumped wildly, and her mind was in riot as she tried to process what had just happened between her and Alex.

She could tell—as she finished her list of qualities that she wanted in a man—that he'd taken himself out of the running, and she understood why. Cam had enlightened her earlier. *He doesn't do commitment, Jess. Never has, never will.* Carried away with his encouragement, she'd ended up describing someone quite different from Alex English. But as she watched him withdraw, something sharp and painful in the vicinity of her heart made her panic.

It had been forward and impulsive to ask Alex to dance, but desperation had muddled her senses, making her cross a line. If he was going to walk away from her, if she wasn't going to see him again while she was in Philly, she wanted one perfect moment in his arms before she lost him to a sea of eager women.

As they danced, he'd changed his mind about a friendship. So had she.

Despite the fact that she had agreed to be friends, it was a lie. It was utterly impossible for her to be his friend now. She wanted him like a heroine wants a hero, like a lover wants her beloved, like a woman wants a man—she wanted his heart and his soul and his body.

She picked up her drink and finished it, mewling softly with longing as she felt the imprint of his warm lips brushing against her cold hand. Jessie clenched her eyes shut, unable to forget his warm breath against her ear, the strong muscles of his back under her fingers, the burn of his eyes as they looked into hers, the touch of his lips to the back of her hand. If they hadn't danced, she could have just gone on *imagining* what it would be like to be with Alex, but now she had a taste, and that taste had unleashed a terrible hunger inside her.

She turned to enter the ballroom, but still deeply lost in thoughts of Alex, she didn't see Cameron waiting for her just inside. When his hand reached out for her wrist, she almost dropped her martini glass.

"Cam!" she hissed, giving him a surprised look and grasping the thin glass stem in her fingers.

Several people turned around, and one person shushed them.

"I think it's time for us to go," he growled softly.

Jessie looked just beyond Cameron to Alex, who stood about ten feet away, his eyes focused with fury on Cam's back. She was certain that Cam and Alex had just exchanged angry words, and it didn't take her more than a minute to figure out that if Cam didn't let go of her wrist, Alex was going to get involved. She didn't want that. Wrenching herself away from her brother, she frowned at him.

"You're making a scene. Stop treating me like a child."

He bent his head to her ear, speaking through clenched teeth. "We're leaving. Now."

As Cam started for the nearest exit, Jessie found Alex's eyes still focused on her, his lips tight and angry.

"Are you okay?" he mouthed, and she nodded, giving him a slight, reassuring smile and mouthing "I'm fine" before following her brother out the door.

Five minutes later, Jessie sat beside a seething Cam in a taxi.

"I can't believe you were alone with him. Did he touch you, Jess?"

"I'm not answering that."

"Damn it. He is *trouble,* Jessica. Your reputation will be—"

"Mine! My reputation will be and is mine!" She shifted in her seat to look at her brother with fury. "And you can't tell me what I can and canno—"

"I'm your older brother who loves you. Don't pursue it!"

She tried a different tack, making herself calm down and speak in a level, gentle voice.

"It was nothing, Cam. Nothing," she said, tapping her fingers on the windowsill as they stopped at a red light. "The ballroom was warm so I went outside, and Alex joined me. It was just a conversation with an old family friend."

"An old fam—Damn it, is that how he spun it? Don't be naïve, Jess. You're a girl. And you're pretty. That's all Alex requires to seduce someone, and I've even seen him drop his standards on *pretty* now and then. Not to mention, in his eyes, you're fresh meat, and there's nothing Alex likes more than to be first in line."

"You're overreacting."

"He will *screw* you and *leave* you. If you have any feelings for him, your heart will be left *broken*. What don't you understand about that scenario?"

"How it's any of your business."

Cam whipped his head to her. "If I hear he touches you? It won't just be me who gets involved in your business, Jess."

She knew exactly what he was saying. In addition to Cam, who was the third of her four older brothers, there was also Brooks, Preston, and Christopher. None would take it lightly to hear that she was spending time with Alex English. She chewed on her bottom lip.

"I think you're being unfair," she said, as the car started moving again. "What if—and I'm only speaking theoretically here—I dated Stratton or Weston English? Would you have a problem with that?"

"Strat and Wes are not Alex. And to be clear, I like the English brothers. Hell, I consider Alex a good friend. Always have. But he's not for you, Jess. He's not good enough for you."

We'll be discreet, or we can't be friends.

"Maybe he *could* be." Her voice was meek and miserable when she responded. "People can change."

"Jessica!" he said, turning to face her as the car stopped in front of his apartment building. "What the hell is going on in your head? Let go of any fantasy that involves Alex English right now because he's *not* going to change. He. Is. A. *Dog.* A manwhore. Other guys call him the Professor because he could school any of us on getting laid. He's a master at casual, love-'em-and-leave-'em-style sex. And he is absolutely, positively off-limits to you." His eyes skewered her. "Are we clear?"

"You're not my father," she said softly, looking down at her lap, her breathing sharp and ragged.

Cam raised his eyebrows at her, then reached into his pocket and took out his phone. *Hardball.* "Okay, fine, Jess. Let's call Brooks. He's the closest thing you have to a father. Let's see what he thinks."

Brooks was their oldest brother, eleven years older than Jessie, and Cam was right: after their father passed away, Brooks had become the closest thing she had to a father. She knew what Brooks would say about Alex, but more than anything, of all her brothers, she simply couldn't bear to let him down or disappoint him. Brooks was a demigod in Jess's world, and she loved him too much to be at odds with him if there was any other way.

She put her hand on Cam's wrist.

"We're just *talking*. You don't have to call Brooks."

Cam continued to stare at her, hard and angry, poised to hit the send button.

"Please, Cam. Don't call Brooks. There's no need. I *hear* you. You don't approve of Alex English."

Cam gave a few dollars to the driver and slid out of the cab, with Jess following behind. "You shouldn't even *want* somebody like that. You should have more respect for yourself. Don't get taken in, Jess. You're sweet and young, and you haven't lived here in years. I'll tell you what, you want to date an English brother? Sure, go for Wes. He's just about your age, and he's a nice enough kid. But *not* Alex."

As adorable as Weston English was, Jess's heart was already taken, and she knew it. She smiled weakly at her brother as he ushered her into the building. "You worry too much, Cam."

"You're my only sister, Jessica. I love you. And honestly? I like Alex too. I'd hate to have to kill him."

As they stood quietly in the elevator together, Jessie heard Alex's voice in her head.

Jess, if the offer's still open, I'd like to be friends.

She heard the words as clearly as if he was standing beside her instead of Cam, and she sighed. The surrender in his voice? The conflict? The yearning? She'd heard it all. He seemed dead set on not tarnishing her reputation by association, and she understood that he was fighting a battle within himself by even agreeing to spend time with her. Knowing that he was struggling not to want her should have taken the edge off her own hunger, but it didn't. If anything, it only made her want him more, because it proved—on some level—that he cared for her.

It was a very bad idea to see him on Tuesday, even under the now-laughable guise of friendship. He'd be pitting his natural instincts against some sense of honor he felt for her. And she'd be using all her strength to keep from reaching for him, knowing that the shame of compromised morals and a broken heart would be her only reward for giving in to her desires.

And yet her heart thrummed wildly, begging her not to cancel, not to pass up a chance to spend a little more time with him. It urged her to keep her date, to be his friend—if that's all he could offer and all she could accept—to get to know him again and find out if the sweet boy she'd so cherished as a child was still living and breathing somewhere inside the womanizing playboy he'd become.

Chapter 4

When Alex woke up on Saturday morning, the first thing he thought of was Jessie Winslow's body pressed up against his as they danced to "The Way You Look Tonight." He'd dreamed of her for most of the night—her sweet smile, her red lips, the bright green eyes that had darkened as he held her in his arms. She affected him like no woman ever had, making him weak and wanting, making him wish for something he shouldn't have. Jessie was openhearted and innocent. Her words about him—*I know exactly who you are*—touched him in a place he barely knew existed, making him feel like he'd been biding his time with other women, just waiting for her to grow up and come home.

And now she was here, and her brothers would beat him to a bloody pulp if they knew the direction of his thoughts. How much he wanted her in his bed, writhing under him, crying his name as he made her come over and over again.

He grimaced because, although he wanted her, he couldn't allow her to be another conquest. Not Jessica Winslow. He cared about her too much to allow that tawdry outcome to their reunion. Having her in his bed simply wasn't possible . . . because Alex had shied away from commitment since he was seventeen years old, and the only way he'd touch Jessie was if he was somehow able to offer one.

Her words haunted him with sweetness, planted like seeds in the fallow, forgotten earth around his heart: *Kindness. Respect.*

Two qualities Alex wasn't exactly known for. He frowned as Johanna Martinson's face flitted though his mind, her seventeen-year-old cheeks tear streaked and devastated when she learned that Alex had cheated on her. But it wasn't just the distressing, disturbing memories of Johanna that bothered him, but of the many women whom he'd bedded and discarded since, never calling again after saying he would.

Someone who makes me laugh.

He closed his eyes, relaxing, his own lips tilting up as he thought of her laughing over his awful pickup lines. Though making someone *come* was what he did best, making Jessie laugh had felt just as good in its own way, and the realization surprised him.

Someone smart and interesting.

Alex was smart. He knew it, and everyone else knew it. He was the acting CFO of English & Sons at twenty-nine, an almost unheard-of confidence in someone so young. And interesting? Well, she had certainly *seemed* interested, he thought, the memory of her eyes, engaged and seeking, bolstering his confidence. That was something, wasn't it?

A little daring maybe. Someone who surprises me in good ways.

He smiled, thinking of all the ways he'd like to surprise her, how much he'd like to see her eyes darken with pleasure or brighten with wonder because he'd thought of something special to do just for her.

Someone who lets me put my cold feet against his warm legs.

The thought of Jessica naked beside him in bed, entwining her legs through his was enough to make him groan as his body responded to the fantasy, growing harder and longer under the sheets.

Someone who makes my toes curl when he kisses me.

His breathing became ragged as he reached down to touch himself, rubbing his hand over his straining flesh as he closed his eyes, throwing his head back against his pillow, hearing the sweetness of her voice in his head.

Someone who can't take his eyes off me.

When she'd turned around in the lobby, when she'd entered the ballroom last night, when she'd found him at the bar, when he'd found her on the balcony . . . every time, he'd been powerless to look away. His only aim was to drink in the beauty of Jessica Winslow, unable to see anyone else but her, unable to—to—

He cried out softly in his bed, flexing to the point of pain, before his body released the tension within, pulsing rhythmically on his stomach in wet, blissful waves. His hand fell limply to his side as he shuddered and trembled. His heart thumped wildly as he realized that his orgasm had been fueled almost entirely by a woman he'd barely touched, a woman he barely knew, a woman who was already so far under his skin, he woke up thinking about her, his body demanding release at the very thought of her.

Someone who chooses me. Only me.

Without thinking, he picked up his phone and canceled tonight's date with Rebecca Everhardt. He sent her a quick text, without explanation and without a plan to reschedule. Then whipped the covers off his body and stalked to the shower, letting the hot water pelt him as he rested his head against the glistening white tile. Maybe he'd go into the office today and try to get some work done—Barrett was all over him about a possible merger with an international shipbuilding company, and he had yet to run the numbers.

His eyes widened as he realized he was actually considering going to the office.

On a Sunday.

What was happening to him?

Alex didn't work on weekends—weekends were for fun. For parties and picking up random, beautiful women and lots of sex. And Alex didn't cancel dates. Not with Rebecca, anyway. She was a wildcat in bed, a filthy talker, adventurous to the point of extreme, suggesting things that porn stars might object to. Before last night, hers was the one date he'd actually been looking forward to, hopeful that a little bit of Reckless Rebecca would leave him too exhausted to feel empty.

He leaned his head against the shiny white shower tiles and closed his eyes as hot water beat against his back. *I know exactly who you are.*

She didn't, of course—regardless of her Facebook research and Internet searches. She didn't know him at all.

He had sex with a minimum of five different women every week. He went out on "dates" mostly for the short thrill of the hunt and the endgame of getting laid. He didn't commit to any of the women he banged, though he knew this hurt their feelings. He enjoyed what they offered, yet remained unattached and put the onus of their disappointed expectations back on them. He'd learned with Johanna not to get emotionally involved, and he'd never made that mistake again.

Jessie Winslow didn't know the first damn thing about who he was. He was a womanizing cad. A country club manwhore, as Margaret had so bluntly pointed out last night. He was someone who used women for his own pleasure without a care for their reputations or feelings.

What shocked Alex the most, as he rinsed off and wrapped a plush, white towel around his waist, was that when he thought of Jessica, he wondered what it would be like to be the man she was looking for. Last night, when she told him she knew who he was, she looked at him with trust and warmth—like maybe he wasn't just the millionaire playboy the rest of the world saw. He kept rolling her words around in his head, wondering what it would feel like to be the person who warmed her feet, curled her toes, and never looked away.

Reaching up to rub his chest reflexively, he realized—with no shortage of wonder—that the expected ache wasn't there. He was thinking about a woman in terms that went beyond a casual fuck, and he didn't feel terrified. In fact, he felt . . . good.

It all boiled down to one striking, unexpected truth:

Jessica Winslow made Alex English want to be a better man.

Alex's office door swung open with a crash, and he looked up to see his older brother Barrett standing in the doorway, holding a golf club and ready to attack.

"*What the hell, Barrett?*" Alex demanded, leaping from his chair.

Barrett's face went from fierce to shocked to incredulous in a matter of seconds. "What the hell, *Alex*? What are you doing here? I thought you were a prowler!"

Alex plopped back down in his seat, looking at his desk, which was littered with spreadsheet printouts. "Um . . . working?"

"It's *Sunday*," said Barrett, placing the golf club against the wall by the door and sitting down in one of the two guest chairs in front of Alex's desk.

"Yeah. I know."

"I've never seen you here on a weekend. Never."

"Well, now you have."

"Aren't you usually out to brunch with last night's bed-fellows right about now?" Barrett raised an eyebrow and smirked.

"Yeah." Alex took a deep breath and sighed, throwing a pencil on his desk in frustration. "Hey, can I talk to you?"

"What about? The Harrison–Lowry merger?" Barrett flicked his eyes to the spreadsheets on his brother's desk. "I *knew* there could be a potential snag going British with this one. I said as much when we—"

"Barrett."

"What?" Barrett's blue eyes finally connected with Alex. "Huh?"

"Nothing's wrong with the Harrison–Lowry merger. Lowry is being one hundred percent cooperative. Can you just be my brother for a minute?"

Barrett sighed deeply, looking disappointed. "What's her name, and how much do you need?"

Alex rubbed his jaw and shook his head. "Nothing like that."

"Oh. So no one's faking a pregnancy, stalking you, looking for compensation after buying a wedding dress, black-mailing you with compromising pictures, or sending their ex-military boyfriend to kill you over an unauthorized bed-room video?"

As much as Alex hated to admit it, these were all valid concerns on Barrett's part. Every scenario had played out at least once in Alex's life, and some more than once.

"Nothing like any of that. Different situation."

"Different how?" said Barrett, looking skeptical.

Alex bit his lip. "I need advice."

"About . . . ?"

Alex swallowed, shifting uncomfortably in his seat. "A girl."

Barrett leaned back, looking utterly confused. "*You* want *my*—"

"Advice about a girl." Alex repeated, holding his older brother's eyes. "And please stop being an asshole about it."

"I have to admit, I'm a little fascinated. You're—you're the *Professor*, Alex. If anyone knows women, it's you. I mean, you could teach a master class on banging—"

"Forget it." Alex pursed his lips, looking back down at his desk and taking a new pencil from the cup beside his computer screen.

"Alex." Barrett's voice was firm and gentle. "Talk. I'm listening. What do you need?"

Alex took a deep breath and looked back up. "Have you ever been friends with a girl? Like, not slept with her, or, um, even *tried* to sleep with her? Just been friends?"

"Can I ask who we're talking about?"

"Not yet. I need your answer first."

"Okay. Um, yeah. At Penn I was friends with a few girls who I didn't sleep with. And I'd consider myself friends with Daisy. And frankly, even though I sleep with Emily, I'd consider her my *best* friend."

"Take Emily and Daisy out of the equation. They're practically family."

"I *could* . . . but you know? When you're friends with a woman? Really *good* friends? She can almost feel like an extension of your family."

Alex mulled this over for a second. In his mind, he separated the women of his life into two places. His mother, Emily, and Daisy lived in a place reserved for the women he loved and respected. And it occurred to him that although Jessica wasn't his family, it felt more organic to group her with them than with the dozens of other women with whom he spent time.

"Alex, I've never seen you like this. Who is this girl? Hope Atwell?"

"You're joking, right?"

"Margaret Story?"

"No. I never even sealed the deal with Margaret."

"*Really?*" Barrett's surprise was justified. Alex *always* sealed the deal. "Then who?"

"Jessica Winslow."

Barrett's mouth dropped open, his eyes wide. After a beat, he shook his head, as if disgusted or disbelieving. "I know that you are *not* talking about Jessica Winslow, the baby sister of Brooks, Preston, Chris, and Cameron Winslow."

"She's in town for a few weeks. Just for the holidays."

"And you have a death wish by New Year's?"

Alex winced.

"Have you lost your mind?"

Alex squirmed in his seat.

"*Clearly*, you have." Barrett rubbed his chin, then scoffed lightly, shaking his head. "If you even *look* at her, they will *kill* you. They will. *Literally*. Kill you."

"Thanks," muttered Alex.

"Shall we take a walking tour of the hallway?" Barrett hooked his thumb toward Alex's office door.

Just outside Alex's door, in the corridor of English & Sons, framed pictures of local regattas, polo matches, and cricket games covered the cream-colored walls. One of the largest and most impressive pictures was a photograph of the four Winslow brothers, shoulder to shoulder, holding a massive silver cup at the 2012 Philadelphia Polo Championship.

The perennial victor at every conceivable gentleman's sport, Brooks had actually been on the U.S. Olympic sailing team and placed third at the 2000 Olympics in Sydney. And Preston, who was an old rival of Fitz's when they were at college together, had crewed on the national rowing team in 2008 until he tore his rotator cuff and was no longer able to compete. As for Christopher and Cameron, both were top-notch polo players like their brothers, and formidable squash opponents. But in lieu of the sportsman life as a profession, both had opted for business, and English & Sons regularly engaged in ventures and partnerships with C & C Winslow Ltd.

Alex didn't need to go on a corridor tour to know that the Winslows were fit and fierce. He'd stared at the photo for at least twenty minutes this morning. All the brothers had the same coal-black hair as Jessie's, and all had different shades of green eyes, though none shared the crystal-clear emerald green of their little sister.

"The Winslows are professional athletes, Alex. They are *made* of muscle. Muscle, muscle, and more muscle. That's it. And they will pummel you to a pulp if they find out you're going near their sister."

"I know."

"And we do business with Chris and Cam. Regularly. They're getting into bed with us for this Harrison–Lowry shipbuilding deal in England. The Winslows have dual citizenship, which will expedite all our red tape. I was even thinking about asking Chris to head up the merger over there."

"Again, not news to me, Barrett."

"Jesus, no wonder you're acting so weird." Barrett shook his head, his eyes serious, almost grave. "Alex, listen to me: you know hundreds of girls. Thousands. Find someone else."

Alex stared back at Barrett, his mind replaying the loveliness that was Jessica last night in the moonlight. *Someone who chooses me. Only me.*

"You must let this go," said Barrett gently but firmly. He folded his hands in his lap, looking at Alex with uncharacteristic compassion. "You've been popular with the ladies for as long as I can remember. And I know that Philly's tagged you as the playboy of the English clan, and I know that quite a lot of what's said about you isn't true. I know this because I've cosigned most of the checks that bought you out of situations that were loud and distracting, but also fabricated. As far as I know, you haven't gotten anyone pregnant or promised to marry anyone. And those pictures we bought? You were asleep in them."

Alex didn't say anything, but Barrett was right on all counts. He was careful about using protection, he'd never proposed to anyone, and while pictures and video had been taken of him, he'd never actually taken any of his own.

"But Alex, you've never done anything to mend or rebuild your reputation. If anything, you've encouraged it. Leaving high-profile parties with a different woman than the one you walked in with. Taking two girls for brunch on a Sunday morning wearing the same dresses they were wearing the night before. Smirking like it all might be true when asked by reporters, instead of defending your name. You're not a bad person, but you've allowed the rest of the world to believe you are a complete cad. And while that might make you the edgy darling of the society pages, it makes a nice girl like Jessica Winslow off-limits."

Alex swallowed, then clenched his jaw, staring at his desk and feeling frustrated and a little bit miserable.

"Which is why I can only be friends with her."

"Which is why you should stay away from her."

"I *can't*," Alex insisted in a low, tortured whisper.

"Why?" asked Barrett, shaking his head. "Why her?"

Because she looks at me the way everyone looks at you.

Because she sees something good in me when everyone else sees a one-night stand.

Because my chest stopped aching the moment my eyes locked on hers.

"Because she asked," he finally answered.

"She asked to be your friend?"

Alex nodded.

"And you . . . what? You can't just say no? She's been in England for a decade. It's not like you have an attachment to her."

Alex's mind flashed back to her wild, black hair tumbling around the popped collar of a pink polo shirt, bright green eyes wide and trusting as they locked on his. "Can I be on your team, Alex?"

"Maybe we have history."

"History."

Feeling frustrated, Alex cocked his head to the side and narrowed his eyes. "You know, Barrett? You fell in love with the gardener's daughter when you were eight years old. Would it be so impossible for you to believe that something like that could have happened to me with Jessie Winslow?"

Barrett's face softened at Alex's reference to Emily, but his eyes were still concerned. "Do you truly want to be her friend?"

No, growled his body.

"Yes. I swear it. Her friend. That's all."

"You're not going to try to get her in bed?"

Alex shook his head. As much as Alex wanted Jessica in his bed, he truly intended to keep their relationship aboveboard.

Barrett took a deep breath. "You can't spend time with her if you're having Thursday nooners with Hope Atwell and banging Sally, Molly, and Mary on the side."

"Done. I'll end things with Hope and clear the rest of my calendar."

Barrett looked truly shocked. "Just like that? You'll throw over Hope and the rest of your social life to be *friends* with Jessica?"

"She's only here for five weeks. I can go back to my old life when she goes home." Even as he said the words, they felt bitter in his mouth. He rubbed his chest for a moment, returning his eyes to Barrett for advice.

"Okay." Barrett's voice was still worried, but more thoughtful now. "If you're really serious about this, here are some suggestions. When you're with her? No hotels. No tinted-glass limos. No drunken groping on the dance floor of nightclubs where anyone could get a photo on their smartphone."

"Got it."

"You don't hold hands with a friend or try to get her alone in dark corners."

"Okay. Lots of don'ts. What *can* you do?"

"You can meet in public places for breakfast or lunch and go your separate ways in separate cabs when your meal is over. You can kiss on the cheek to say hello. And otherwise? You talk."

"Talk."

"Talk and maybe laugh, if that feels right, and eat lunch together. I don't know. Talk about all that history you two have. Ask her about London, where she went to school, and what she does for work. Come to think of it, ask her about Devon and see if she knows anything about the shipbuil—"

"Barrett," Alex said sharply.

"Right. You know what? Forget she's a woman, Alex. Just be her friend."

Alex sat back, taking a deep breath. Forget she's a woman? Forget the sky's blue. Forget the grass is green. Forget the onyx black of her hair and the red rosiness of her lips and the—

"*Friends*, Alex," said Barrett meaningfully, watching Alex's face. "And what exactly are you going to do about the Winslows?"

Alex sighed loudly. "The proof will be in the pudding. If my behavior is above reproach, they won't have anything to worry about."

"God help you," said Barrett, standing and pushing in the guest chair. "If you hurt a hair on that girl's head, God help all of us. We're no slouches, but English brothers against Winslow brothers? We'd lose."

Alex watched as his big brother headed out the door, then turned his chair to the Philadelphia skyline. Hurt her? He'd die before hurting her. He'd die before watching that trusting light go dark in her eyes.

For the first time in his life, Alex knew . . . if anyone was going to get hurt, it would be him.

By ten o'clock on Tuesday morning, Jessica was a wreck.

She and Alex hadn't exchanged phone numbers, nor had he called her at Westerly to reconfirm their lunch date, which made her fear the worst. Maybe the scotch and the moonlight had momentarily addled his brain, and upon further reflection he had decided that there was no way in hell he was interested in a friendship with Jess when there were thousands of willing females ready to please him.

Alex didn't *do* friends, right? Her brother said it and Alex said it—and regardless of their brief, sweet history as children and blatant attraction to each other as adults, there was no reason for her to think she was the exception to that rule. Her heart clenched painfully as she wondered if she'd be stood up.

"More's the better," she declared crisply, thinking of her brothers, who'd be a massive complication to her "friendship" with Alex.

From the very *un*subtle comments her brothers had made at Sunday dinner about Alex—Preston coughing the word *manslut* every few minutes was especially delightful—she knew that Cameron had shared the news of her balcony rendezvous. She hadn't confirmed or denied, or even acknowledged, their suspicions, but it was amply clear that if they found out she was spending time with Alex, the proverbial shit would hit the proverbial fan *tout de suite*. And since they all moved in the same social circles and their family estates were next door to each other, keeping their friendship a secret would be next to impossible.

"So, good. He didn't want to be your friend in the first place. He's probably not sending a car anyway. You haven't a thing to worry about."

She snapped her laptop shut and shoved it across her comforter, looking at it with distrust and disdain.

Jess was so ridiculously infatuated with him, she'd made a major tactical error. She'd spent all of Monday and a few hours of Tuesday morning surfing "Alex English" online.

She'd kept up with Alex's colorful and prolific dating life over the years, of course, but from the distance of England and the improbability of ever knowing him again, she could review the news and accompanying photos with a lot of fascination, a good bit of wistfulness, a little bit of voyeurism, and a pinch of defensiveness. Back in Philly, after a dance in the moonlight, with a lunch date on the table (maybe), it was harder to feel removed from Alex's shenanigans.

There were several stories about women claiming he fathered their children, though when she cross-referenced these claims with "DNA testing," none came up with any verification. There were women moaning and crying about Alex promising them things: cars, jewelry, apartments, a wedding. All these women made their claims loudly and bitterly, then disappeared soon after, leading Jessica to assume they were paid to stay quiet, and wondering—as many others did—if payoffs were an admission of guilt or just a way to silence false claims against the English name. There were several other dramatic stories that included pictures of Alex asleep in boxers, and one of his bare ass aired out for all the world to see. Sighing, Jessica grudgingly admitted she had looked a little longer at those pictures than was necessary to ascertain his probable lack of consent.

Cameron had described Alex as a dog and a manwhore, and yet, despite the fact that Alex was obviously a prolific womanizer, with no evidence of ever having had a short- or long-term girlfriend, Jessica couldn't quite accept that description as the sum and total of his character.

She leaned back against the pillows on her bed, her face softening with yearning as she thought about Saturday night. He'd been so concerned, so conflicted about her offer of friendship, as though even sharing a lunch with him could somehow hurt her reputation or her heart. Despite her obvious attraction to him, he had looked deeply into her eyes and refused to take advantage of her. More than once he insisted that he wasn't any good for her, and she'd seen the regret on his face when he assessed how different he was from what she was looking for.

How could she reconcile the Alex she knew with the man splashed all over the Internet? With the man her brothers were so passionately against her dating?

She kicked the laptop with her foot and hopped out of bed, crossing the plush, pale pink carpet of her room to her dressing table, which had a full skirt covered with pink cabbage roses. She sat down on the puffy stool and looked at herself in the same mirror she'd stared into all those years ago when Alex was a freshman heartthrob at St. Michael's Academy and she was a third-grader at Miss Thoroughgood's Prep. For hours she'd stared at her face—at her crooked, pre-braces teeth and freckled nose—before going downstairs for their bon voyage party. That was the night Alex English kissed her on the forehead and whispered "'No Girls Allowed' doesn't mean you" in her ear. That was the night she'd lost a piece of her heart.

And since seeing Alex on Saturday, she felt that lost piece within her grasp—in the warmth of his presence, in his teasing grin and bright blue eyes. She knew what people said about him, and she'd even read the accounts with her own eyes, but it didn't seem to matter. It didn't matter that he'd been with scores of women. It didn't matter that they claimed he'd treated them poorly. It didn't matter that her brothers objected to her seeing him. It didn't matter that spending time with him might ruin her reputation in Philadelphia.

Seeing Alex again, talking with him, dancing together—it had all served to remind her of how important he'd been to her once upon a time. And despite his reputation, he felt no less important to her now. If she'd doubted the strength of her childhood crush, meeting him again on Saturday night had confirmed it. Her feelings for Alex were still alive, and no matter how much he had changed, a part of her would always belong to him.

That was why—with her heart racing but her head held high—she went to her closet to choose an outfit to wear to lunch. She cared for him. She wanted him. And until he gave her a reason not to, she resolved to trust him.

Ninety minutes later, she sat in the front parlor at Westerly, ostensibly reading her Kindle, but anxiously flicking her eyes to the window every few minutes to see if a hired car was making its way down the driveway.

"Why, Jessie," said Olivia Winslow in her crisp British accent, wandering into the parlor and smiling at her only daughter. "I thought you'd gone into town."

"No, Mummy. I'm . . . just reading. Though I may head in for lunch in a bit."

Her mother grinned, which brightened the sharp lines of her thin face. "Lovely idea! I'll come with you. We can go to the club or to—"

"No!" Jessie's Kindle fell to the floor with a loud crack as she lurched forward. She leaned down to retrieve it, then looked at her mother helplessly. "I, um, I might have a date. With a friend."

"You *might*?"

"I *do*." She nodded, handling her Kindle uneasily.

"You *do*?"

"I *think* I do." Jessie bit her lip, casting a quick glance to the window and wincing when she found the driveway still empty.

"This friendly date wouldn't be with a certain English brother, would it?"

Jessie stood quickly, smoothing her simple black dress and placing her Kindle on the seat behind her. "Mummy . . ."

"Cameron has been in a tizzy. And if Preston doesn't stop cough-mumbling *manslut,* he's going to be hoarse."

Jessie's face flushed, and she looked down at the folded hands on her lap. If her mother wanted to give her a lecture about Alex, she would . . . politely . . . not listen.

"What time is Alex sending a car?" she asked gently.

"Noon," Jessie answered.

"Well, it's only 11:55. May I wait with you?"

Jessie took a deep breath and nodded, shoving her Kindle aside and sitting down again. Her mother took the seat across from her, farther from the window, but facing the driveway.

"Oh, here's some news. I just got off the phone with Eleanora English. She invited us for Thanksgiving dinner, to welcome us home. I hope you have no objections to my accepting her invitation."

"None at all."

Despite her calm reply, Jessie's heart leaped at the thought of seeing Alex on Thursday. And then she berated herself because if he failed her today, she had no business being happy to see him on Thursday. She snuck a glance at the empty driveway.

When she turned back to her mother, Olivia's expression was thoughtful.

"I imagine it's not always a picnic to have four older brothers."

"I love them."

"Of course you do, pet," said Olivia, running a hand through her sensibly short, grayish-blonde hair. "But we fare rather well on our own, don't we? At Harrell House? Back in London? At least we did until you got that little flat."

She grinned. "We do just fine, Mum."

"Then will you take my advice and be brave? Don't let them boss you around. Not about anything, and certainly not about your heart. Stand your ground, right? I like to think I raised my daughter to be just as strong as my sons."

"Easier said than done. There are four of them. One of me."

"Then do it four times as often so they know you mean it. To be clear, I'm not just talking about Alex. I've heard all the rumors, and honestly, pet, I'd rather see you date—"

"We're not dating—we're just friends," she said way too quickly.

Olivia searched her daughter's face before smiling at her with compassion, like she could see into Jessie's heart and knew exactly how much of it was owned by Alex English.

"All I mean to say is that it's up to you to choose whom you spend your time with. I love my four boys, but you're going to have to carve out your own place in this family. You might want to start with not letting Cameron yank you out of parties when he has a fit of protectiveness."

"He was so angry with me. It was overwhelming."

"You haven't lived with them for a good part of your life, and I suspect that you want to please them now that we're all together for a spell. I might suggest that you"—she smiled gently at her daughter—"*love* them, but *please* yourself."

Nodding, her heart swelled with gratitude for her mother's wise and gentle counsel. Jessie had, more or less, already come to the same conclusion, but having her mother's support made everything feel better. "Thanks, Mummy. I'll try."

Olivia stood, tall and smart in black slacks and a gray cashmere sweater, and turned to leave the room. "By the way, your *friend's* car just pulled up. Have a lovely date, pet."

Chapter 5

Lacroix at The Rittenhouse was Alex's go-to restaurant when he wanted to impress a date, but he had purposely gone another route, respecting Barrett's advice that he shouldn't be seen at a hotel with Jessie, even if their only purpose in being there was to share a meal as friends.

There was only one other place that kept asserting itself as a choice, and Alex finally surrendered and made a reservation at The Dandelion. With its inviting fireplaces, country manor décor, and an ample selection of British libations, he was hopeful that Jessie would feel right at home.

However, sitting in front of the fire as he waited for her, he had misgivings. The Dandelion wasn't very posh or exclusive. It was quirky, but comfortable, with its mismatched, plaid-upholstered armchairs and ploughman's lunch— nothing more than an upscale pub, really. And even though it was Alex's favorite restaurant in all of Philadelphia, he'd never taken a date there. If Jessie didn't like it? Well, that would tell him something about her, and make it a hell of a lot easier to say good-bye after their lunch.

Because he was determined to say good-bye.

He couldn't have possibly canceled on her after accepting her offer of friendship, and with the Winslows joining the Englishes for Thanksgiving, it would have been terribly awkward to cancel Tuesday only to see her on Thursday. But Alex cared about Jessie in good and unfamiliar ways, in all the *right* ways that felt so new to him, and he couldn't expect her to accept his history blithely and associate herself with him out of a misguided attempt to pay back a childhood kindness. Cam was right. She was way too good for him.

"Mr. English?" asked a waiter. "Miss Winslow is here."

Alex stood quickly, lifting his eyes to hers, and felt it again—the way the ache in his chest eased as he looked at her face. He didn't feel slick and debonair as he took her hand. He felt helpless. He felt out of his depth.

As if she knew, she smiled like the sun, and moon and stars rose in his eyes, and for just a moment—just a split second—an elusive fantasy unfurled in his mind, and he recognized the sharp, astounding joy he'd feel if Jessie Winslow actually belonged to him.

"Alex," she said, squeezing his fingers.

"You look beautiful, Jess," he said softly, without an ounce of artifice, his words uncharacteristically earnest. She wore a simple black dress under an unbuttoned tan raincoat, her shiny, black hair in a low ponytail that trailed softly around her neck to rest on her shoulder. She looked casual but lovely, and his heart throbbed just from looking at her. Despite Barrett's advice, he stepped forward to press his lips against her warm cheek. He felt it all the way to his toes—the rush of something wonderful just outside his grasp. She smelled of tea rose again, and Alex breathed deeply, lingering, hating like hell to ever draw back from her.

Hearing her lovely, light chuckle near his ear finally forced him to lean back and smile into her shining eyes.

"Best hello kiss ever," she said, just a hint of a British accent peppering her speech.

His chest swelled as he searched her eyes, and when she squeezed his fingers again, he realized he was still holding her hand. *You don't hold hands with a friend or try to get her alone in dark corners.*

"I hope it's okay that I reserved a table for us beside the fireplace? It's well lit," he added hastily, letting go of her hand.

"It sounds charming." She grinned, taking her first look around the pub-like restaurant, resting her hand on the Stewart plaid of the love seat where Alex had been sitting. "I love it here. How did I never know there was a perfect slice of England in the heart of Philly? And how clever of you to choose it for us."

He couldn't help putting his hand in the small of her back as the maître d' showed them to their table, and Alex savored the contact of helping her with her coat. Was it creepy that he inhaled through his nose as he drew it away from her? He didn't care. She smelled too good not to enjoy it.

Once they were settled across from each other, with a blazing fire before them, Alex finally started to relax. Jessica perused the menu quietly, and he wondered if she was as nervous as he was, and then he realized how awesome it felt to be nervous around a woman. It had been years—more years than he could count—since he felt like he wanted to put effort into a date, since he felt the sudden rush of excitement to touch the hand or cheek of a woman. It was like reacquainting himself with a part of his life long forgotten.

"What?" asked Jess, her eyes suddenly capturing his over the top of her menu. "Do I have something on my nose?"

"No," he said, shaking his head. "Sorry. I'm staring."

"Yes, you are," she said, looking back down at her menu.

You talk, Barrett had said. *So talk, Alex!*

"What do you think of London?"

"I love it," she said, still looking carefully at the options before her. "It's home."

"What do you love?" he asked, his own menu forgotten in his lap.

"Hmmm. The weather . . ."

"The weather?" he demanded. "Rainy and gray?"

She still didn't look up at him, but her eyes crinkled from smiling. "Yes, I love the rain. But there are plenty of bright, sunny days, and with the exception of deep summer, it's always pretty cool. And timeless. And lovely. Since I adore traveling, it's also the perfect home base for discovering the rest of Europe. What's not to love?"

"You love to travel?" he asked her.

"I do. I adore it."

"And what else do you do there?"

"Socially?" she asked, still looking down.

"Sure, that too."

"Too?"

"I was actually asking about your work."

"Guess," she said, smoothing her hair with one hand as she continued to stare at her lunch options.

"Jess . . . is there a reason you're not looking at me?"

She did. And it happened again—the helpless feeling that didn't hurt. He felt his smile fading, and his eyes widened, searching hers desperately.

"That's why," she murmured, looking back down, her cheeks high from her beaming smile. "Because you can't handle me yet."

"Ha!" he scoffed, sitting back in his chair. "*I* can't handle *you*?"

"Nope. You get flummoxed every time I look at you."

Damn it, she was right, but his ego wouldn't let him drop it. "You do realize I'm a worldly twenty-nine to your tender twenty-three?"

"Yes, I do. Which is why it's so amusing."

"I've been around the block, Jess."

"So I've heard. Around and around and around."

"I *can* handle you, Jess."

"Really."

"Uh, yeah. Really."

The challenge in her eyes was unmistakable as she slowly lowered her menu, and he braced himself, leaning into her beauty, into her smile, into the memories of her as the child who'd adored him. As she raised her eyes, he finally forced himself to accept it: she was Jessie Winslow, she was home, she was all grown up and so beautiful, he almost couldn't believe she was real, but she was here having lunch with him so it must be true.

"There we go," she said gently. "Now you see me."

How did she do this? Anticipate him? Comfort him? Somehow reach into his heart and soothe something that had been chafing for weeks? From the moment she'd turned around on Saturday night, it was like a missing piece of Alex was restoring itself—a piece that fit perfectly, that never should have been taken away from him. A piece that he would never have been able to replace on his own, no matter how many other pieces he'd tried to force into its place.

The not-so-awful helpless feeling encroached . . .

"Jess . . ."

"Keep guessing what I do."

. . . and abated. He grinned, thinking about her crossing the ballroom on Saturday night. "A party planner."

"No."

"Am I hot or cold?"

"Warm. I love parties so much, but I wouldn't be a good planner. I'd want to enjoy myself instead of work."

"So . . . something more solitary so you don't get distracted?"

"Now you've gone to the other extreme!"

"Okay. Not *totally* solitary. Or maybe the work is solitary, but the environment is social?"

"Warmer. I'm impressed."

"I'm very smart," he said, winking at her. "And interesting."

"Clearly," she said, grinning that wonderful, open smile that captivated him so much.

"Okay. So you're surrounded by people, but what you do is solitary."

She nodded, and her ponytail bounced up and down, the ends probably tickling the back of her neck. His fingers curled and released in his lap, wishing they could fist in that soft hair or brush against that warm skin, following the curve of her neck to the base of her throat with trembling, reverent fingertips.

"Guess again," she insisted, not letting him get distracted.

"A librarian."

"No."

"Warm?"

"Very."

"Hot, even?" he asked in a low, flirtatious voice, because he couldn't help it.

"Yes," she murmured as she stared back at him.

A waitress stopped by their table and broke the electric moment. Jessie smiled warmly at her, ordering the bangers and mash with a pint of cold British ale. He said "Same," barely looking away from Jessie for a moment.

"A waitress," he said.

"Respectable work, but not mine."

"Librarian was warm?"

She nodded.

"A library is like a . . . museum. Are you a curator? No. A docent!" He knew—somehow *knew* for sure—that he was right.

She rewarded him with a beaming smile and clapped softly. "Impressive!"

"Where?" he asked.

"At the Tate. I volunteer, for now. Hoping for a paid position at some point, once I've proved myself."

"Modern art," he said, cocking his head to the side. "I wouldn't have guessed that."

"Why is it such a surprise?"

"I don't know. You seem traditional."

"I *am* traditional, but I love modern art. The edginess of it, the way it breaks the box and shatters the ceiling."

"Will you hate me if I say I don't get it?" he teased.

"I wouldn't begin to know how to hate you, Alex," she said gently, searching his eyes with a small smile. "But . . . I think we should take a field trip together so I can educate you on everything wonderful there is to get about modern art."

"To the Tate? Long field trip."

"Maybe someday to the Tate," she said with a grin. "But for now, just to ICA at UPenn."

She was referring to the Institute of Contemporary Art at Alex's alma mater, the University of Pennsylvania. He'd never been. He was too busy splitting his time between girls and studies at college. Not to mention, modern art had never been one of Alex's interests, something he was suddenly anxious to remedy.

"I'll show you what I see," she continued. "And maybe you'll find something you get."

"If you get it, I'll get it," he said, surprised to find he meant it. He wanted to see through her eyes and appreciate something she found beautiful. In fact, he might stop at a bookstore on the way back to the office and see what he could pick up on modern art, just so he'd be ready to impress her a little. "Tell me when you want to go."

"Sunday," she said. "After brunch."

He laughed at her audacity. If she followed his reputation on the Internet, as she had said on Saturday night, she knew about his Sunday brunches. He decided she was teasing him and played along.

"Oh! Are we having brunch on Sunday?"

"Mm-hm," she murmured confidently, looking away from him to smile at the waitress when she returned with their beer.

She couldn't be serious, could she?

Alex leaned his elbows against the table as soon as they were alone again. Despite the fullness of his heart when he was with Jessie, he still had a firm grip on right and wrong, and being seen for Sunday brunch with Jessie was not an option. He needed to set her straight, on the off chance that she was actually serious.

"I can't fall for you Jess," he reminded her. "And you can't fall for me."

She lifted her beer to take a sip, but before she did, she gave him a small, sympathetic smile. "Too late."

Jessie knew that she was being forward, but she couldn't help it. Talking to her mother this morning had given her the final drop of courage she needed to make her move. She let the cool beer stream down her throat, watching his surprised face. There was no use pretending she just wanted to be friends with Alex, because that's *not* what she wanted. She wanted far more from him. Everything she'd ever felt as a child had been picked up with unerring precision the moment her eyes locked with his on Saturday night. She wanted Alex. There was no way around it.

Before he could start pulling away from her again and telling her what a bad influence he could potentially be on her life, she placed her glass back on the table and asked conversationally—as though she hadn't just admitted that she had fallen for him—"So, tell me about English & Sons. What do you do there?"

He took a quick sip of his beer, huffed once, and stared at her with deeply furrowed brows. She could see him mentally deciding if he should argue with her about her feelings or let it go for now. She was relieved when his face relaxed, and he sat back.

"I'm the CFO."

"The numbers guy," she said, tilting her head to the side. "Now who's surprised?"

She gave him a saucy grin. "Bet it comes in handy when you're calculating your stats with the ladies, *Professor*."

He tensed, looking away. "I can't change my history, Jess."

"Alex, I was just joking."

He shook his head. "I know you were, but it's still true. A lot of what they say about me is true."

She reached across the table and covered his hand with hers, watching his face as he flipped his hand so that they were palm to palm. His thumb and fingers curled over the back of her hand, clasping it gently, adjusting and readjusting his fingers until every part of her skin was flush with his.

When he finally looked up at her, he looked so lost that she had no choice but to grin back. "I told you that you couldn't handle me."

He didn't smile back. "Doesn't it bother you?"

"That you've been with a lot of women?"

He nodded.

It did bother her, of course, and when they finally spent the night together, it would bother her in myriad other ways she'd hardly dared to explore yet. But what Jess knew, and Alex didn't seem to understand, was that her heart had already chosen him long, long ago. It didn't matter what had happened in his past as long as he chose her to be his immediate future.

"I'm not exactly a virgin, Alex."

"What does *that* mean?" he asked, his fingers tensing around hers as his face hardened a little.

"It means I'm twenty-three years old. I'm not one for casual flings, but I've had boyfriends and lovers."

He winced, taking a deep breath. "It makes zero sense that I hate knowing that."

She ignored the pleasure she felt from his comment and finished what she wanted to say. "Our histories are irrelevant to now, to here, to this conversation. How many people we've slept with before today really doesn't matter. We can't change it, and I don't know about you, but I really wouldn't want to. The people I've known—and loved—made me who I am today. So, no, it doesn't matter to me that you've had a lot of partners, not in any meaningful way."

"How can that be true?" he asked as his thumb stroked the pad of her thumb distractedly.

"Because our experiences help shape who we are, but they don't define us."

"I doubt your brothers would agree."

She drew her hand away from his and watched as his face betrayed how much he disliked losing that connection with her. "Maybe it's just best for me to lay my cards on the table, Alex."

"Jess—"

"No. Just listen. Here it is. I'm here for five weeks. That's it. Five weeks. And then I go home to my museum and my modern art and my friends and my travel and my life. But while I'm here, I want to be with you. N-not just as your friend, but if that's all you can offer, I'll take it." She shrugged, hoping she appeared more collected and cool than she felt on the inside, which was a tangle of nerves, begging every force in the universe for Alex not to turn her away.

His eyes were brilliant blue, trained on hers like he couldn't look away from her if he tried, so she continued in an uncharacteristically nervous rush.

"I don't care what my brothers think. And I don't care what *your* brothers think. I don't care that you've slept with a lot of people. All I care about is not wasting this chance to spend time together, to pick up the thread from our childhood and see what happens next."

She calmed the trembling of her hand before raising her glass to her lips and taking a long sip of beer. He watched her in silence, his eyes deep and serious.

When she replaced her glass and he still hadn't spoken, she looked at her lap, starting to feel ridiculous. "If that isn't what you want, then let's just drink our beer and eat our bangers and say good-bye . . ."

She was running out of courage. He hadn't given anything away, and she'd laid her heart bare to him. Taking a deep breath, she started to wonder if she'd gravely misjudged this situation and if he somehow still saw her as the child who used to follow him around during flashlight tag, unable to really see her as a full-grown woman. The idea made her eyes burn, and she reached for her purse, readying herself for a hasty good-bye, and knowing that she'd have to be quick because disappointed tears wouldn't be far behind.

The light pressure of his fingers under her chin forced her eyes to meet his. His glance was so hot, so resigned and sweet, that her breath shredded and caught.

He shook his head lightly. "You take my breath away, Jess."

"Then we're even."

"Five weeks," he said softly.

"Five weeks."

"Okay," he said. "For five weeks, I'm yours."

She gasped in surprise, her mouth widening instantly into a happy, relieved smile. Then, without thinking, she leaned across the little table and pressed her lips to his.

Alex's eyes shuddered closed as his blood surged, hot and fierce, in reaction to such unexpected sweetness. Her lips were warm and soft, brushing lightly across his, as though sealing their deal. His fingers scrambled on the table between them, reaching forward to find her hands, which were braced flat against the wooden surface, and he curled his fingers around them. Tilting his head slightly, he caught her top lip between his, kissing it gently over and over again, catching it and releasing it, nibbling tenderly, as he memorized everything about this stolen moment with Jessie.

She represented everything sweet and innocent from his happy childhood. She was an injection of something fresh and new when his life felt so flat and empty. For the first time in ten years, he'd just made a commitment to someone, albeit temporarily, and it shocked him to realize how good it felt. He was bewildered by his reaction to her, stunned by the depth of his feelings, grateful to feel so alive, like maybe—just maybe—he could someday be worthy of someone as lovely as Jessica Winslow.

Alex was accustomed to much steamier, sloppier, more invasive kissing, but Jessie's gentle caress held more promise, more hope, more, more, more—so much more risk for his heart, it made his body weak and desperate. It made him wonder how to balance his longing for her with his fears about ruining her.

Squeezing his fingers, she drew back from him, pink cheeked and beaming.

"I've wanted to do that for fourteen years," she said, wiggling one of her hands away from one of his to pick up her pint glass and take a sip.

He laced his fingers through her remaining hand, letting go of his worries for now, grinning back at her. "So what's on the agenda from now until Christmas?"

"You tell me." She shook her head with wonder. "Five weeks with Alex English. What should we do?"

Amazingly, he didn't flinch or internally groan at her use of the word *we*, as he almost always did when a woman used it in reference to herself and Alex. Somehow coming from Jess it felt okay, and Alex decided he'd take any beating the Winslow brothers wanted to mete out if it meant that he could have five weeks with their sister.

"Thanksgiving on Thursday," he said. "And I'm sitting next to you so I can hold your hand under the table."

He chuckled lightly as she nodded.

"My brothers are taking their fiancées to a Christmas tree farm on Saturday. They invited me to join them, but I said no."

"Oh! Say yes. *Please* say yes. I'd love to go. My brothers and I cut down our own every year at a Christmas tree farm in South London, and I'd miss it if I skipped out this year."

"Okay. I'll tell Emily yes, as long as you *don't* invite your brothers."

"Deal." She grinned over the rim of her beer glass. "It'll be nice to see Emily again. I remember her very well."

"Were you two friends?"

She shrugged. "Not really. Emily went to Haverford Elementary, and I went to Miss Thoroughgood's, so I didn't see her very much. But, you know, there was the odd Saturday afternoon when we'd ride bikes on Blueberry Lane or play Barbies under the weeping willow at Haverford Park. The Story girls were older and the Rousseau twins spent every summer in Paris, so there weren't many other little girls to play with."

"Sloane Ambler?" asked Alex, with a twinkle in his eyes.

"Sloane." Jessie's nose twitched, and her eyes narrowed. "Ugh. My nemesis."

"I actually remember that—how much you two disliked each other. You were always bickering."

"We were years younger than you! I'm surprised you noticed."

"Dash Ambler was one of my best friends. I was over at Green Farms all the time, and . . ."

"And?"

He grimaced, then smiled sheepishly. "God, I hope this doesn't sound creepy, but I always sort of had my eye on you."

"Are you kidding? You're fulfilling every one of my pre-teen fantasies right now by confessing that. I might faint."

The waitress came back with their lunches, and Alex let go of Jessie's hand regretfully to dig into sausage and potatoes.

He flicked a glance at her and grinned. "Any other unfulfilled fantasies you want me to tackle?"

He'd meant the comment to come out lighter than it did, but as soon as the words left his mouth, the entire atmosphere between them changed, tightening, tensing, charging, catapulting them from memories of their shared childhood on Blueberry Lane to the present day, where they'd just agreed to spend the next five weeks getting to know each other exclusively.

She raised her eyes, which were dark and deep, and her voice was low and direct when she answered. "I can think of a few if you're offering."

Alex tried to ignore the downward rush of blood that made him instantly hard under the table. Images of Jessica in his bed pervaded his brain and made it almost impossible to think of anything else. He forced his mind away from the image of her naked beneath him, and somehow managed to put together a coherent thought.

"I shouldn't have said that."

"Why not?"

"Because I have rules about you, Jess. I need to be a gentleman with you. For the first time I can remember, I want to be good. I want to treat you—I don't know—differently, I guess. But I'm a *little* out of my comfort zone, and I'm a *lot* weak for you."

Could she possibly understand? Could she understand how desperately he didn't want to ruin whatever was growing between them? How important it was to set her apart from the other women he'd been with by treating her with care and respect? Did she have any idea how long it had been since he felt this way? He couldn't bear to jeopardize it by thinking with his body instead of his head, even though it was new for him.

"You *are* good," she finally murmured in defiance.

"No, I'm not. I'm—"

"You *are*," she repeated, reaching for his hand and bringing it to her lips for a gentle kiss. "You'll see."

"Jess, please—"

"But I understand. I'll . . . I'll behave myself."

With an uncertain, lackluster smile, she released his hand and turned her attention to her lunch. Alex watched her, wishing he knew how to do this better, wishing that he had more time than a miserly five weeks to get it right.

Chapter 6

The rest of their lunch had included small talk about their families and careers, how Jessie had turned out to be the least athletic of the Wild Winslows and how Alex had a real and true passion for the financial work at English & Sons, not just a familial obligation to the firm. When it was time to say good-bye, he pulled her into a cloakroom behind a curtain just inside the entrance of the pub and put his arms around her.

Jessie sighed, leaning against his chest and letting her eyes close slowly as she sensed his warring feelings—wanting to touch her, yet desperate to shield her from any gossip that might materialize as a result of their agreement to spend time together.

She rested her cheek against his shoulder, wrapping her arms around him as he leaned his forehead down into the curve of her neck, as if resting there for a moment, gathering the courage to walk away from her. His hair tickled her skin, and he breathed deeply, his chest pushing into the place where her heart throbbed, strong and insistent, for *him*. She shushed her longings, amazed by how far they'd already come and determined to let Alex move at his own speed.

She was very touched by what he'd said about wanting to treat her differently, but Jessie's acquiescence to moving slowly had far more to do with her wanting to support him than actually believing that he'd ever hurt her.

Jessie was young, but in addition to her natural intuitiveness, living abroad had helped her refine her skills of reading people, understanding them; the psychology of the people around her wasn't the challenge to Jessie that it was to most other people. She understood Alex—that he saw her differently than the other women he'd enjoyed in his life. She understood she was somehow precious to him. But at the same time, she didn't want Alex to idealize her, which is why she'd shared that she wasn't some lily-white virgin to be placed on a pedestal. She was a woman fully grown, and she knew what she wanted.

"I don't want to let you go," he muttered.

"Fine with me. We can set up house in this closet. You, me, lots of coats . . ."

He leaned back and opened his eyes. "What time are you coming over on Thursday?"

"Four o'clock, I think."

He nodded. "Bump into me at the bagel shop in Haverford on Thursday morning. I'll be there at eight."

"A secret assignation." She grinned. "Okay. But I can't promise I'll be alone."

"I don't care. We can act like strangers if you want. I just want to see you. I'll be dying by Thursday morning."

The words slid off his tongue, warm as honey, and Jess gasped lightly, flicking her glance to his lips and licking her own, wishing she could taste him.

"Stop," he said in a low, breathless voice, dropping his forehead to her shoulder again.

"Then don't say things like that."

He released her suddenly, taking a step away. She saw the frustration on his face, the internal battle. "Thursday."

Jessie nodded, and he turned on his heel. From behind the curtain, she heard the door of the pub slam in his wake, and her whole body relaxed, slumping against the wall behind her. In the quiet of the little room, her phone buzzed. She fished it out of her purse, swiping at the screen to read the new message.

I miss you already.–A

—

You could have kissed me good-bye.–J

—

No, I couldn't have. I wouldn't have been able to stop.

—

Maybe I don't want you to stop.

—

You're killing me, Jess.

—

Hurting you isn't what I have in mind, Alex.

—

Jessie slipped out of the pub, and the car that Alex had arranged was waiting at the curb. The driver rushed around to get the door for Jessie, and she stepped inside, ducking to avoid the light rain.

As soon as she was settled, with her seat belt buckled, she eagerly looked at her phone.

But I am terrified I will hurt you.

Her heart dropped, and she took a shaky breath as she read the words over and over. Did he mean that he cared for her but feared his reputation would tarnish hers? Or did he mean that the idea of spending time with her frightened him because he was afraid she'd get attached and he'd end up letting her down?

She started typing a response, but she couldn't seem to get the words right—to reassure him, to comfort him, to let him know that she wasn't afraid. In the end, she didn't write back at all, returning her phone to her bag, and watching Philadelphia whiz by as they headed for the Main Line.

"I'll take two poppy seed, two cinnamon, two sesame seed, and—what kind does Dad like?" Alex asked Weston.

"The smelly kind," said Wes, without looking up from his phone.

"Oh, yeah. And an everything bagel, please." He turned to Wes again. "What do you think the Edwardses like?"

"Are they coming for breakfast?" asked Wes.

"No. I thought I'd drop off a bag at the gatehouse."

"Hold on," said Wes. "I'm searching 'pregnant person bagel.' Maybe they crave a certain kind."

Good idea, thought Alex, rubbing his chest as it tightened uncomfortably.

Every year, on the Wednesday night before Thanksgiving, Eleanora English ordered pizza for dinner. She said it was something her mother had done every year of her childhood and, though it felt strange to see the pizza deliveryman approach their mansion every year, every English brother loved the tradition as much as their mother.

Last night, as they washed down pepperoni and sausage pizza with cold Sam Adams, Daisy and Fitz made their announcement. Daisy was seven weeks pregnant, and Fitz beamed at his family as he shared that they'd just heard their baby's heartbeat on Tuesday. A brand-new Edwards–English baby was on the way, arriving sometime in early summer.

As the conversation dissolved into tears and laughter and congratulations, Alex had swallowed uncomfortably, the ache that had been absent since his lunch with Jessie reasserting itself. Fitz was going to be a father. It was almost unbelievable.

"Okay. Don't get Daisy poppy seeds. They'll show up like drugs when she pees in a cup."

"Way more info than I needed, Wes."

Alex turned back to the young woman behind the counter, who looked like she was about to faint as she looked back and forth between two of the handsome, legendary English brothers. Alex winked at her and grinned when she gasped softly.

"And another dozen mixed, please, but no poppy seeds."

"O-okay," murmured the teenager, staring at him, unmoving.

"Whenever you have a sec."

"Oh, right!" she turned her back to him and started counting out the bagels as Alex flicked his eyes to the door. Still no Jess. He sighed loudly.

"What?" asked Weston.

"Nothing."

"Surprised you came home last night. Was sure you'd have a hot date."

"I like pizza before Thanksgiving."

Weston shrugged. "Can you believe Fitz and Daisy? Are *you* ready to be an uncle? I'm not."

Alex clenched his jaw. He was happy for Fitz and Daisy, really he was. It just felt like everything was changing too quickly.

"I don't know," said Alex honestly, paying the bagel clerk and waiting for his change.

"You want kids, Al? Someday?"

Alex's chest throbbed as he took his change and thanked the clerk, but as he turned to leave, he was distracted by the little bell over the front door of the bakery. His eyes cut to the entrance, and his whole body felt the sudden impact of sharing the small shop with Jessica.

His chest relaxed, as though on her command. He felt the smile on his lips as he watched it echo across hers, tilting her beautiful red lips up in a sweet hello. He knew how those lips felt between his, and his body suddenly hardened in remembrance, his heart beating faster as her grin swelled, reading his mind.

"Hey, Jessie. Preston," said Weston, taking a step toward their neighbors. "Brooks, it's been a long time. It's good to see you."

Alex's eyes left Jessie's face in a rush, suddenly noticing Brooks and Preston Winslow standing behind their little sister, their expressions grim and focused solely on Alex. It seemed that Cameron had given his older brothers a warning about Alex's interest in Jessie.

Brooks was two years older than Barrett, which meant he was five years older than Alex, and though they'd never been friends, Alex had spent a lot of time with Cameron and Christopher while growing up down the street.

Preston was Barrett's age, though it was Fitz with whom Preston had a fierce crewing rivalry. During Preston's senior year at UPenn, sophomore upstart Fitz had—for a brief few weeks, until Preston corrected the matter—shoved Preston's name off the top of the intercollegiate charts with his fast and furious rowing times.

Brooks offered Weston a tight smile, taking his proffered hand. "Wes. You're looking good, kid. Still riding?"

"Absolutely. You?"

Brooks nodded. "Want to join me on Friday morning?"

"Sure," said Wes. "I'd like that."

"Jessica will join us too," said Brooks, laying a hand on his sister's shoulder, then raising his green eyes to Alex. He nodded coolly. "Alex."

"Brooks."

"I'm sorry, I can't," said Jessie, patting her brother's hand but holding Alex's eyes. "I already have plans."

"What plans?" asked Preston.

"Plans that aren't any of your business," said Jessie in a firm but gentle voice, looking at Brooks before walking away from her brothers, past Alex and Weston, to get in line.

"Do *you* have plans, Alex?" asked Brooks, his eyes boring into Alex's with a sharp warning.

"I do."

Actually, he didn't. He wondered, feeling an unfamiliar rush of jealousy, whom Jessie was seeing tomorrow.

"Not with my sister, I hope."

It didn't matter that Alex was lying about having plans tomorrow. The reality was he wasn't interested in answering to Brooks, or any other of the Winslow brothers, about his social life, whether it included Jessica or not. He didn't intend to misuse or hurt their sister, and yes, they had a right to feel cautious about Alex, based on his dating history. But if Jessie was going to be a part of his life, even temporarily, he needed to make it clear that whatever was happening between them wasn't anyone else's business.

Alex turned his head to look at Jessie, who stepped to the counter to place her order, before looking back to Brooks and Preston.

"I guess if I did, that would be my business, Brooks. No offense."

"We're going to have a problem if you don't stay away from her."

Alex nodded slowly, taking a deep breath. "We might have a problem, then."

Preston stepped closer until he was shoulder to shoulder with his older brother. "Leave her alone, *Professor*. She's not going to be a notch in your bedpost."

Alex stared at the wall of muscle mass and furious frowns that were Brooks and Preston Winslow, and felt his own temper rising.

"Don't talk about Jessie like that. Even if it's within the context of her spending time with me."

"Are you going to school me on how to treat women respectfully?" asked Preston, taking a step closer to Alex and fisting his hands. "And here I was, under the misguided impression that your particular *skill set* lay somewhere else completely."

Weston, who suddenly seemed to understand what was going on, took his place beside Alex. Though Wes wasn't as intimidating as Stratton, he wasn't small either, and Alex appreciated the show of support.

"Back up, Pres," said Weston quietly.

"Stay out of it, kid. This is between us and Alex."

"Wrong." Jessie had suddenly reappeared, standing between Brooks and Alex, with her bagels in one hand and the other on her hip. Her lips were pursed and angry as she shook her head at her brothers. "It's between *me* and Alex."

"Jessica Fairchild Winsl—" started Brooks in a low voice.

"No," she said in a fierce whisper, lest they attract more attention than they already had. "You will *not* get involved. I am an adult, and this is my personal life, Brooks. There's no room for you in this equation." She turned to Alex, and Wes and gave them an apologetic smile. "Please tell your mother how much we're looking forward to seeing her later?"

Alex nodded, wishing he could take her in his arms, and to hell with the bloody Winslows. No one was going to tell him he couldn't date Jessica Winslow. If they tried it, Alex would mete out a punishment of his own.

But his eyes, so hard and angry, softened as they swept over her face. "We'll see you a little later."

She sailed out the door, and her brothers followed behind, but only after Brooks gave Alex a look that made his feelings entirely clear: *If you hurt a hair on my sister's head, I will* kill *you.*

Jessica looked around the living room of Haverford Park, enjoying the clamor of conversation as Englishes, Winslows, and Edwardses reacquainted themselves with one another. Alex stood across the room, talking animatedly with Barrett, Fitz, Cameron, and Christopher about the upcoming shipbuilding deal they were all working on, and Jessie loved darting glances to her brothers, who finally appeared to be getting along with Alex.

After the scene that Brooks and Preston had *almost* made at the bagel shop, Jessica had shared some harsh words with them on the ride home.

"How dare you behave that way! Shame on both of you!"

"Alex English is trouble, Jessica," said Brooks from the driver's seat beside her, but his voice wasn't quite as strong as usual. She suspected he was surprised by her anger and chagrined by her response to his behavior.

"Then he's *my* trouble, not yours!" Her mother's words encouraged her and made her stronger as she pushed back against her brothers. "I've never been so embarrassed. And you, Pres! A *notch* on a *bedpost*? Oh, you didn't think I overheard that? Well, I did. *Christ!* Alex was more respectful of me than either of you!"

"I was only being honest. And if you get tangled up with him, then you're going to get what you deserve," said Preston belligerently from the backseat. "Alex is with a different girl every night."

"*Get what I deserve*? Do you think so little of me? Do you think I disrespect myself so much that I'd willfully spend time with someone determined to hurt me? Do you trust me at all?"

"We trust you," said Brooks in a calming voice. "We don't trust *him*."

"Give him a chance," she spat out, crossing her arms over her chest and staring out the window until they got home. She went straight to her room and didn't come downstairs again until it was time to go to the Englishes' house for Thanksgiving dinner.

"Barrett says you're only home until Christmas?" asked Emily Edwards from beside her. Though Mr. English's excellent champagne flowed freely, Jessie noted with some amusement, and a little bit of admiration, that Emily was drinking a beer from the bottle.

Jessie looked away from Alex and her brothers and smiled warmly at Emily. "Yes. We head home the day after Christmas."

"Do you mind my asking why you're spending the holidays here this year?"

"I don't really have a good reason. We generally spend Thanksgiving at our ski house in Vermont, and my brothers cross the pond for Christmas. This year, Mummy suggested Haverford. Possibly because Cam and Chris are in the middle of a big deal with your fiancé. I think it's just easier to stay in Philly this year."

"Lucky for us," said Emily, "because we get to see you. You know, Daisy and I—and my roommate, Val—get together every Thursday for a girls' night at Mulligan's near Penn. Want to join us next week? We'd love to have you."

Touched by Emily's kindness, Jessie reached for her hand and squeezed it. "I'd love to."

Emily leaned a little closer. "I hear you and Alex are coming with us to get his Christmas tree."

Jessie beamed at the sound of his name, flicking her glance to him and catching his eyes. They burned over the rim of his old-fashioned glass as he took a sip of scotch. He was so handsome in his light blue oxford shirt, navy suit, and tie, her heart skipped a beat every time she looked over.

He grinned before reengaging in the conversation with their brothers.

"I—I hope you don't mind that we're coming," she said, forcing herself back to her chat with Emily.

"*Mind*?" Emily looked up at her cousin, Daisy, who reentered the room looking pale and tired. "You okay?"

Daisy sat down on Emily's other side, dabbing at her lips with a tissue. "Oh. I'm okay. Just, um . . ."

"Water?" asked Emily.

Daisy shook her head. "It'll settle. It just takes a minute."

Emily turned back to Jessie. "Daisy's expecting."

Jessie's eyes widened as she looked down at Daisy's flat stomach, then back up at her face.

Daisy explained, "The doctor says the first few weeks can be a little rough, but it's actually a good sign."

"Congratulations," said Jessie. "How's Fitz doing?"

Daisy turned slightly to look over at her fiancé, who seemed to sense her glance and caught her eyes, mouthing "Are you okay?"

Daisy nodded before turning back to her cousin and Jessie, placing her palms gently over her belly. "He's doing great. Fitz and I have a long history. This baby was unexpected, but very wanted and very loved already."

"Daze, I invited Jessie to join us next Thursday—"

"Oh! Great!"

"And she asked if we minded that she was coming on Saturday."

Daisy scooted forward on the sofa, leaning over Emily's lap to move closer to Jessie. "Truth?"

Jessie nodded, leaning forward too, until she and Daisy were almost touching foreheads across Emily's lap. "Truth."

"We were *shocked*," confided Daisy.

"You were?"

"Of course!" exclaimed Emily in a dramatic whisper, making both Daisy and Jessie look up at her. "Alex doesn't bring dates to anything family oriented! He keeps his social life totally separate from his family life."

"Until now," added Daisy. "What's going on with you two?"

Jessie leaned up, glancing over at Alex, who was deep in conversation. "Truth?"

"Truth!" hissed the cousins.

"I've *always* had a thing for Alex English."

"So has at least half of the female population in Philly," observed Emily. "But you're the first one for whom Alex appears to have a thing, too."

Jessie couldn't help the pleased chuckle that escaped her lips.

"You have to tell us more!" insisted Emily.

"Next Thursday," promised Jessie, getting up to use the ladies' room. "I promise more *truth* at girls' night."

Alex watched Jessie giggle with his future sisters-in-law, pressing a finger to her lips to say "shhh" before winking at them. She caught his gaze—just for a split second—as she left the room, and it was the only hint Alex needed.

He'd been waiting for an opportunity to get her alone, but he couldn't exactly bolt across the floor and follow her to the powder room, could he? He threw back the rest of his scotch and then gently shook the lonely ice cubes.

"Anyone else need a refill?"

Barrett, Fitz, and the Winslow brothers shook their heads distractedly as Alex edged away from the group and disappeared into the butler's pantry. Though it looked like a small, enclosed nook in the corner of the room, Alex knew that if he pulled a secret lever behind the sink, a slim panel opened into a back hallway. As quickly and quietly as possible, he exited through the panel, racing down the long hallway until he reached the double doors that entered the kitchen. He waved cheerfully at his mother's caterers before launching himself through the swinging doors that led to the grand dining room, sliding across the slick parquet floor, and exiting into the main hallway of the house. He ran a hand through his hair before careening around a corner toward the powder room. Just as he approached, the maid's closet opened, and he grinned to see Jessie's face peeking out of the crack. Her fingers grabbed his sleeve, pulling him into the darkness, and his body slammed back against the door, closing it firmly.

"Jess," he panted.

"Took you long enough," she teased.

It occurred to him to say so many things to her under the cover of darkness.

I can't stop thinking about you.

I can't think about anyone else.

I've never felt this way before.

As his eyes adjusted to the pitch black of the closet, he stepped forward, reaching out his hand. It was rescued by hers, her palm pressing softly against his in the darkness, and he shifted just slightly so that they could lace their fingers together.

The closet smelled of lemon-scented furniture polish and tea rose, and Alex breathed deeply, knowing that it was the smell of heaven, and when Jessie was gone, it would be the smell he searched for in his head to remember a perfect moment.

"Alex," she whispered. "Kiss me."

His heart, which was sprinting from his race to the closet, caught for a moment before he pulled her closer.

"Jessie."

Her palm lighted on his chest, resting over the throbbing of his heart before sliding up to his throat, her fingertips fluttering gently against this skin of his neck as they rose to his cheek. Her palm finally stilled, resting against the warm skin of his face.

"It's okay," she murmured, taking a step closer to him so he could feel the shallow raggedness of her breathing against his chest.

She's nervous too, he realized, reaching out to wrap his arm around her waist and pull her closer. Dropping her hand, he curled his other arm around her so that they were finally flush, her chest pressing to his, her heart racing with his, her lips waiting for his.

"Five weeks," he said, breathing in the smell of tea rose and the sweetness of her breath so close to him.

"I'm yours," she answered, returning the words he'd used at lunch on Tuesday to seal their agreement to spend time together.

The simple words were infinitely more intimate and arousing than the dirtiest, filthiest things that had been whispered into his ear a million times.

"Jess," he groaned.

Bending his head swiftly, Alex let his lips land flush and full on hers, parting softly as she opened her mouth. She sighed with pleasure, and he tightened his grip around her as her fingers curled against his cheek with urgency before sliding under his ear to meet her other hand at the back of his neck. They laced there, tightening as he found her tongue, stroking the slick, wet heat with his. Jessie arched her back, a whimper released from her throat. Alex's hands slipped to her lower back, and he pushed her more firmly against him so that she'd feel how hard he was for her, how much he throbbed behind the thin barrier of his pants, how much he wanted her.

She rolled her hips against him, which blew his mind, and he trailed his lips down her throat, brushing them against the hot skin of her neck as she gasped softly.

"Jessie, Jessie," he murmured, kissing and licking, branding her with his lips as her hands slid into his hair, flexing and releasing against his scalp and telling him how sensitive she was to his touch.

"Kiss me again," she panted, and he rushed to comply, fiercely covering her mouth with his, finding her tongue again, sucking on it, laving it, sliding against it in a dance he'd done a million times with hundreds of different women.

Except . . .

This was different. Completely different.

For the first time in Alex's life, sharing breaths and lips and sighs and touches was somehow sharing something far deeper, far more meaningful than he'd ever experienced before. And inside Alex's heart, which had ached and throbbed for weeks, the missing piece that was Jessica Winslow slipped into place. He felt it. He knew it. He had no idea what to do about it, but she lived there now, embedded in the very fiber of his being.

The thought was sobering—absolute in its meaning, which he refused to consider. But he pulled back from Jessie, resting his head on her forehead as their breath mingled in shallow pants between them.

"Who are you seeing tomorrow?" he asked.

"W-what?" she breathed.

"Tomorrow. You said you couldn't go riding with Brooks. Who are you seeing?"

"Oh." She laughed softly, a breathy, happy sound that made Alex drop his lips to hers again to brush against them with agonizing sweetness. "You."

"Me?" he whispered, his lips grazing hers as his mouth formed the sound.

"If you're free."

"Instead of Saturday?" he asked.

"In addition to Saturday."

He searched his head, and his heart, for a feeling of panic to assault him. He'd seen Jessie on Tuesday and twice today. If he saw her tomorrow *and* Saturday, it meant he'd have spent the week with her. It was an unprecedented amount of time to spend with one woman, and no matter how good it felt to be with Jessie, it made him pause. He waited and waited—her soft, pliant body like perfection in his arms—but the panic didn't come. He felt, as he had since the moment he'd found Jessica again, nothing but a sharp longing for more, and an intrinsic peace in having her.

"What did you have in mind?"

Her body relaxed instantly in his arms, and she chuckled softly again. "I need a chauffeur. Pick me up at ten tomorrow?"

"At Westerly?"

"Mm-hm."

"Okay."

He pulled her a little closer, burying his nose in her hair, surprised by how easy it was to let her into his life, into his heart.

"I should go back now before anyone notices," she whispered, and he tightened his grip a little.

"I don't want to let you go yet."

"I think closets may be a new fetish for you."

"Only if you're in them with me."

Jessie touched her lips to his before dropping her hands from his neck. She peeked out of the closet for an instant to be sure the coast was clear, and then she was gone.

And Alex realized, with no small measure of bewilderment and in a totally different way, that he was gone too.

Chapter 7

"*Now* will you tell me where we're going?"

Jessie looked at Alex in the driver's seat beside her. He was dressed in jeans and a blue-and-white button-down shirt under a leather-collared barn jacket. With his dark blond hair and patrician good looks, he was like her own personal Ralph Lauren model, right down to his GranTurismo zooming down her driveway.

"Yes," she said, as he turned onto Blueberry Lane. "One of my favorite modern artists, Cort King, lives just south of Stroudsburg, and he gave me permission to visit the studio at his farm today to check out some of his works in progress."

"Stroudsburg? You want to drive an hour and a half to look at some art that's not even finished yet?"

"Yep. I told you I love traveling," she teased.

He looked over, unable to keep the goofy, whipped smile from taking over his face. "Fine. I'm at your service."

"You might even like it, Alex."

"Doubtful. But I like you, Jess."

Jessie chuckled with surprise. "I like you too."

The Winslows had stayed at the Englishes' house until almost nine o'clock last night, lingering over the most beautiful Thanksgiving dinner Jessie had ever experienced. Seated beside Alex—a coincidence that, she suspected, had been engineered *by* Alex, as her place card was noticeably askew, as though it had been hastily replaced—she held his hand under the table for most of the two-hour dinner, learning the textures and contours of his hand: the deep grooves of his love and life lines, the warmth of his palm pressed against hers.

When they got up to leave, Alex dropped her hand, and Jess flinched inside, the loss of contact more painful than she expected. As she walked home last night beside her brothers, the temporary nature of her time with Alex chafed at her. They'd been reacquainted only for a week, but her feelings for him were growing at an alarming rate. If she didn't preserve some small part of her heart, being torn from him after Christmas would be excruciating.

Jessica suspected that part of the reason Alex was able to set his normal dating rules aside and spend so much time with her was because her visit was finite. She knew that when she left—no matter how sweet and meaningful their time together—Alex would go back to his old ways, probably with relief, and she would return to the life she'd left behind. Alex English didn't do long-term commitment, and she had no right to expect it of him. She reminded herself of this as she glanced over at him again, telling herself that their agreement was for five weeks only, to live in the moment. Nothing would change the fact that he lived in Philadelphia, and her life was in London.

She glanced over at him again, refusing to let sad thoughts steal a moment away from their day together.

"Thanks for driving me, Alex."

"My pleasure. You know, I was surprised your brothers weren't waiting with loaded shotguns when I pulled up."

"For the record, they do *not* like it that we're spending time together."

"You don't say."

"I *do* say. But I also say it's my life to live."

"I have no idea why you're taking a chance on me."

"Yes, you do. You're important to me. I care about you." She took a deep breath and sighed. "Anyway, it's only for five weeks, right?"

He glanced over at her, his eyebrows furrowed and his jaw hard. "Right."

"Can I ask you something?"

"Sure."

"I get the feeling your schedule isn't usually this free. I mean, driving me up to Stroudsburg today at the last minute, and the Christmas tree farm tomorrow."

"I cleared it."

"What?" she asked, her head whipping to the side, her eyes raking his face to ascertain the truth of this statement. Even though she'd asked to spend time with him, she hadn't asked for exclusivity, and he'd never actually offered it.

"When I said I was yours for five weeks, I meant it. Completely."

"Oh." Her heart did somersaults as her mind screamed a warning, forcing her to focus on the words *five weeks*. "I didn't know for sure."

"I said I wouldn't hurt you, Jess. I can't be seen with other women and with you at the same time—it wouldn't be right. So I won't date anyone else or be with anyone else until after you go home. I promise."

"Alex, I never asked—"

"I know you didn't. I want it to be this way. I *need* it to be this way."

His right hand abandoned the wheel to reach for hers. She caught it quickly, pressing his palm to her lips and closing her eyes as he cupped her cheek.

But a bleak question circled in her head, laying the groundwork for heavy-heartedness later. How in the world would she find the strength to walk away from him? And once her feet made the journey back across the sea, how long would she have to wait until her heart finally followed?

Alex could tell that it surprised Jessie to learn that he'd curtailed his robust social life for the few weeks she was visiting. It surprised *him* how organic it felt not only to make the changes in his life, but to inform her of them. She was changing all the rules he'd lived by for years, and it occurred to him to wonder if there was another girl in the world for whom he would have so willingly changed his ways. He couldn't think of another. No one compared with Jessie. No other girl had ever looked at him as she did. It set her apart. It always would.

For the rest of the drive north, they listened to music and chatted companionably about their brothers. Both one of five, they laughed at shared conundrums and marveled over how similar Barrett and Brooks were. They rehashed Preston and Fitz's college rivalry, Jess sharing that for years the Winslows referred to Fitz as Fucking Fitz and Christopher had almost slipped and said it at dinner yesterday. Speaking of Christopher, Jessica reconfirmed what Alex already knew: that Chris, who was closest in age to Jess, was the most sensitive and thoughtful of the bunch, while Cameron was the most hotheaded. Jessica asked whom Alex was closest to, and he answered honestly that although he loved all his brothers equally, it was Weston, more and more, to whom Alex felt closest.

"What about Stratton?" asked Jessie. "He seems mysterious."

Alex took a deep breath. "Strat's . . . different."

"How so?"

"He's good-looking, right?"

"I'd be comfortable saying he's the second-best-looking English brother."

Alex winked at her, nodding in thanks.

"Barrett's just *so hot*," she added.

"*What*?" he demanded, whipping his head to face her.

"Just kidding!" she said, giggling in her seat beside him. "Just kidding. It's you, it's you, it's you."

She said this lightly, between gasps of laughter, but Alex's heart swelled from the words said so guilelessly. She wasn't trying to be sexy. She was just being Jess, and he was being swept away with her a little more every minute he spent with her.

"Glad we got that straight," he said, grinning at her.

"So what's different about Stratton?"

"You'd never know Strat and I came from the same parents. I mean, I—" He stopped abruptly, realizing how blunt he was about to be.

"You what?" she asked.

"I bang anything that moves," he said softly, opting for honesty, but instantly regretful when the words left his mouth.

She gasped, and he glanced over at her, at the stricken look on her face as she stared straight ahead, out the windshield.

"And Strat?" she asked in a thready voice.

"Doesn't." He hated himself for ruining their playful conversation, but the reality of who he was, who he had been for most of his life, wasn't something that would go away if they ignored it. "It's who I am, Jess."

"Not right now," she insisted, looking at him with hurt eyes, even as she defended him. "Right now you're here with me, and we're just . . . talking."

"But my reputation—"

"Doesn't matter to me."

"It should."

"It doesn't, Alex, and no amount of you trying to shock me is going to change that. I don't care how many women you've . . . banged. I only care that you're sitting next to me right now."

He couldn't explain why her answer frustrated him so much, but he almost yelled at her when he demanded, "Why do you only see the good in me?"

"Because I know you. I know your heart and I—I'm . . ." She looked down quickly, swallowing whatever words had been on the tip of her tongue.

He clenched his jaw, looking away from her, trying to concentrate on where they were headed so he wouldn't miss a turn and get so far off course, they'd never find their way.

Could he actually protect her from his reputation over the next few weeks? From the gossip columnists having a field day with her? From ex-lovers sending her hate mail? From well-meaning friends and family warning her away from the depraved sex fiend, Alex English? He felt helpless because he knew he couldn't. If they were going to spend time together, they couldn't pretend his history was irrelevant. She needed to brace herself a little bit, not live in this rosy bubble, pretending he was still the fifteen-year-old boy she had a crush on.

And yet, glancing at her again, at her beautiful face so serious and sad, he couldn't bear to ruin their time together either.

"Hey, Jessie," he said softly, "remember when Cam, Chris, Dash, and I had the cabana band?"

Whereas most children in suburbia had garage bands, Alex and his friends had commandeered the pool cabana at Westerly one summer and made terrible music loudly and often, much to the disdain of the other families on Blueberry Lane.

"Mm-hm," she murmured, still withdrawn, still sad, still not looking at him.

"Every time we played 'Jessie's Girl,' you came running."

A tiny smile played at the corners of her mouth.

"I convinced myself that you were playing it for me."

"We were," he confessed, the part of him that was still fifteen remembering her bright green eyes smiling at him the summer before she moved away. "*I* was, Jessie-girl."

"So skip the middle."

"What?"

She shifted her body a little, turning to look at him. "Skip the middle. Pretend that last week you were playing 'Jessie's Girl' for me. Pretend that I didn't move away."

Just for a moment, the fantasy unfurled in his head. Jessie at fifteen, when he came home from college, cocky and ridiculous from the amount of pussy he was getting. Jessie at eighteen, when his urban manwhore days were just hitting stride. Jessie at twenty-one, looking at him with disgust when his first scandal hit the tabloids.

Suddenly he was relieved she'd moved away, that she hadn't had a front row seat to his debauchery. Then again . . .

"If you had stayed, I might have been different," he said, swallowing the sudden and painful lump in his throat. "I might have been a better man if those green eyes had been watching me, Jessie-girl."

He turned into the gravel driveway of an old farm as indicated by the checkered flag on the GPS. As he cut the engine in front of a pristine white farmhouse surrounded by the largest, oddest metal sculptures he'd ever seen, he turned to look at Jess. Her smile was the sweetest, most tender, most heart-poundingly beautiful thing he'd ever seen, anytime, anywhere, when she said, "They're watching you now, Alex. All they see is you."

The next day, Alex arrived at Westerly to pick her up on foot, explaining that they were riding with Barrett and Emily in

Barrett's SUV, and that Fitz and Daisy, who were coming from their apartment in the city, would be meeting them at the farm. As he took her hand, he was distracted by something behind her, and Jessie looked back to see Cameron standing at the foot of the stairs, his expression hard as granite as he shook his head back and forth.

"Cam," called Alex, still holding her hand. "We still playing squash on Thursday?"

"Screw you, Alex," said Cam, turning abruptly and heading up the stairs. After several steps, he yelled over his shoulder. "Yes. And I'd wear body armor if I were you."

After they were outside, Alex finally let his eyes drop to Jess, sweeping them over her jeans, hiking boots, and cream cashmere sweater. She handed him her bright red pea coat, and he held the shoulders as she shrugged into it.

"He's thawing out," said Alex sarcastically.

"Sounds like a real friendly game," she said, pulling the front door shut and turning around to face him.

Alex buttoned the three large black buttons on the front of her coat, then grabbed two fistfuls of the thick wool fabric and pulled her closer. "He's just worried about you, but he doesn't need to be."

She flicked her glance down his body, resting below his hips for a moment before looking back up and grimacing. "Might want to wear, er, um, *protection* next week. Knowing Cam, I'm fairly certain a lot of shots are going to be taken at your, um . . . parts."

"Though your concern means a lot to me, I promise my *parts* will survive," said Alex, tilting his head to the side in a look that was a thousand percent adorable.

"I dearly hope so," said Jessie. She hadn't met his parts yet, and she wanted them intact when she did. The thought made her cheeks flush and her breathing quicken. "Hey, I dare you to kiss me."

"Right here?"

"Right now."

After viewing Cort King's eccentric sculptures for an hour yesterday, they'd found a country diner for lunch and then headed back to Haverford, enjoying the leisurely ride home. Although they'd held hands near constantly all day, whenever possible, Alex hadn't kissed her again, and their passionate moment in the Thanksgiving closet was starting to feel pretty far away to Jess.

He pulled her just a fraction closer, dipping his head to brush her lips with his. Her eyes closed, and she leaned forward, anticipating more, but when she realized more wasn't coming, she opened her eyes, frowning at Alex's smiling face.

"I wish we were alone right now," he said, shooting an uneasy glance at her front door.

"Not half as much as I do."

"Come for dinner at my place tonight?" he asked, searching her eyes.

"I'd love to," said Jess, her heart pounding as she realized that it would be the first time they were alone in private.

"I'll drive you home after dinner."

"Unless I decide to stay over."

He bit his bottom lip, and Jessie's inner muscles clenched.

"As much as I'd love that . . . no."

"Alex—"

"No, Jess. When you go back to London, it won't be as one of the Professor's Girls. I promised myself."

"Grrr," Jessica huffed, dropping his hand and pulling away from him.

She marched down the driveway without him, toward the arch in the hedges where there was a footpath that led to Haverford Park. As of today, they had only four weeks left together, and she knew he was trying to be chivalrous with her. But damn chivalry. She was getting frustrated and starting to think that she *wanted* to be one of the Professor's Girls for the next few weeks, in *every possible way*.

As she ducked under the arch, still brooding, Alex grabbed her around the waist, and in an instant he had her pushed up against the thick, private hedge, his mouth hot and demanding on hers. She whimpered in surprise, reaching up to plunge her hands in his hair as he lowered his hands to her ass, cupping it roughly, shoving her against his erection which strained against the unyielding denim of his jeans. His mouth ravaged hers, as if starving for her taste, his tongue slipping and sliding against hers insistently as he tilted his head for more access. Jessie arched her back, and Alex bent with her, keeping his pelvis flush with hers, his chest strong and hard against the softness of her breasts, which heaved from the surprise and excitement of such an unexpected, wildly passionate kiss.

He drew back abruptly, panting and stricken as he stared at her. His hands flexed, dropping quickly from her ass, as he took a decisive step back.

"I'm sorry," he whispered in a taut, agonized voice.

"I'm not," said Jessie, out of breath, searching his face with wonder.

"I can't let you think I don't want you."

"I'm reassured," she said. His dark, wild eyes stared back at her. "Do it again."

His tongue slipped out of his mouth and licked his lips, but he shook his head.

Jessie pushed away from the hedge where she was still leaning and reached for the points on his leather collar, pulling him closer.

"Again," she whispered, leaning up to capture his lips with hers.

He waited only a moment before he deepened the kiss, wrapping his arms back around Jessie and sealing his lips more fully over hers. This kiss was gentler and sweeter than the last, his tongue softly stroking hers, making her toes curl as his fingers kneaded her lower back through her coat. After a moment, he broke off the kiss again and lowered his forehead to her neck in a move she was starting to recognize. It was almost as though he hid there from the world, his lashes fluttering against the skin of her throat before closing, breathing deeply through his nose and exhaling warm breath on her neck as he relaxed. Jessie raised her hands to the back of his head, gently stroking the warm skin of his neck, comforting him, loving him, letting him know that he could rest against her for as long as he needed to.

When he finally lifted his eyes, they were soft and tender.

"When Margaret decided to go stag on Friday night, do you know what she said to me?"

Jessie shook her head.

"She said, 'One day I'll say I was there to witness it: the moment the elusive heart of Alex English got sideswiped by a kid.'"

Jessie stared back at him, waiting with baited breath to see what he'd say next.

"She was right," he whispered, his voice almost breaking. "But I don't know how to do this."

Jessie's hands slid to his cheeks, which she palmed gently as she smiled into his eyes.

"You're doing fine," she said.

"This is going to get messy."

"Then let it get messy."

"One of us might get hurt."

"It's worth it to me. Is it to you?"

He nodded, but his face was helpless, and Jessie loved it a little, that he was so undone, because it proclaimed her worth.

"I can't stay away from you, Jess. I just want to be around you as much as possible until you go."

"I want that too."

"They'll eat you alive," he said, shaking his head sadly. "When we come out of a restaurant or go to a party together. They'll take pictures. They'll speculate about who you are, find past boyfriends, they'll—"

"Let them. I have nothing to hide, Alex. And I'm tougher than I look."

"I didn't want this for you. Not *you*."

"Doesn't it matter what I want?"

"Of course, but I—"

"Stop worrying about me."

"I can't. I care about you."

"If that's true, stop putting up barriers between us. Stop worrying about your past. Stop worrying about the rest of the world. Just be with me." She smiled tenderly at him. "You said you were mine until Christmas. So *be* mine, Alex."

"Your . . . boyfriend?" he asked, swallowing audibly after saying it.

"Mm-hm," she murmured, her thumb grazing his cheek softly before she lowered her hands. She ran them down his arms until her hands found his, and he laced their fingers together. "We're already exclusive, aren't we? So what's the big deal?"

"Boyfriend," he said again.

"Yes. Boyfriend and girlfriend." She laughed softly. "They're just words."

He nodded, biting his lower lip and squeezing her fingers. "They won't know what to do with this. Alex English and a . . . a girlfriend. For a whole month."

She beamed. "They'll think you've turned over a new leaf."

"I have, Jess," he said softly, brushing his girlfriend's lips with his before pulling away to look into her eyes. "I promise you, I already have."

Something Alex didn't know: Jessica Winslow was a hundred percent, a total and complete, pain in the ass when it came to choosing a Christmas tree.

She'd turned her nose up at a blue spruce, declaring the light blue color tacky.

Balsam fir smelled divine, apparently, but the weak branches wouldn't hold ornaments, so what was the point?

White spruce had nice, firm branches, she said, but no Christmas smell.

In the end, they chose a Fraser fir, though Jessica pursed her lips and warned him not to put any glass ornaments on the branches, because they'd fall to the floor and break.

What Jessica didn't know was that Alex had no ornaments, glass or otherwise. He had never gotten a Christmas tree for his apartment before. Though he loved Christmas and enjoyed the way his mother decorated Haverford Park, he didn't see much point in decorating his own place. He didn't entertain very much, and it wasn't like he had a girlfriend to take charge. Except . . . except now he sort of did.

A girlfriend.

Jesus, Alex hadn't had a girlfriend since he was a senior in high school, and even then it hadn't lasted long. It was an episode in his life that he tried to forget, but it still seeped into his dreams sometimes. The image of Johanna Martinson's face when she found out that Alex had cheated on her. She'd left school, raced home, drawn a bath, and slit her wrists. Luckily, her older brother, home early from football practice, had walked in. An ambulance was called, and Johanna's life was saved, but Alex had sworn off serious commitment after that. If his actions—his stupid choices—could hurt someone else that deeply, he'd just as soon not raise any woman's expectations ever again.

And yet here he was, breaking all his rules for Jessie Winslow.

Jessie, Emily, and Daisy sat on the side of a hay wagon, chatting, and Alex cast his glance at Jessie, wondering if she knew about Johanna. Probably not. She was only eleven years old and living in London when it happened. And everyone had comforted Alex at the time by reminding him that Johanna's parents were in the middle of a vicious divorce and she was already an emotional train wreck of a young girl. But Alex had known the truth and hadn't really forgiven himself for his part in heaping more pain on her already-hurting heart.

He hadn't seen Jessie coming. And now here she was, all soft and certain, her eyes lighting up to see his, her mouth a goddamned miracle and her body made for loving. And for the first time in over a decade, Alex wanted to use the word *girlfriend.* From the moment he'd seen her, he wanted her, to belong to her, and just a week later, his wish became a reality. She was his girlfriend, and he was shocked and awed to discover that's exactly what he wanted.

"So what's going on with you and Jessie?" asked Fitz, dragging his tree on the ground to stand behind Alex. They were in line for the baling machine, which wrapped netting around the trees for easier transport, but there were at least five people in front of them.

"We're spending time together."

"I was surprised when you invited her today. I can't remember the last time you brought a date to a family outing."

"That's because I don't."

"I'd give you the speech about Jessie being a nice girl and the Winslows killing you if you hurt her, but I have a feeling you don't need to hear it."

Alex pulled the trunk of the Fraser fir forward and dusted his gloves on the front of his jeans. "You're right, I don't."

"So you're serious about her."

"As serious as I can be about someone leaving for London in four weeks."

"Ohhh," said Fitz. "I didn't realize she was leaving."

"This is only a visit. She lives there. She works at the Tate."

"Well, you could always—"

"No, Fitz. She lives there. I live here."

"Well, I guess it makes it easier, huh?"

Alex narrowed his eyes, resenting the implication of his brother's words: *The only way Alex could have a girlfriend is if it was only temporary.* It was probably true, and it made perfect sense, but Alex didn't like it.

Fitz continued, oblivious to the conflict he'd stirred up in Alex's head and heart.

"Well, I hope you don't take this the wrong way, but it's kind of cool to see you hanging out with one girl for a change." Fitz looked over at his fiancée sitting beside Alex's girlfriend. "Daisy and Emily seem to like her. Jessie always was a nice little kid."

She was a lot more than a nice little kid to me, thought Alex, following Fitz's eyes. Jessie was giggling at something Emily was saying, and as she threw her head back, her black waves tumbled down her back, shiny in the sun. His whole body ached in that new, good way that he didn't mind. He'd never seen anything as beautiful in his whole life.

"I'm crazy about her," murmured Alex. Not really to Fitz. Not really to anyone. The words just slipped out of his mouth fully formed. He couldn't have stopped them if he'd tried.

"I can tell."

"You can tell what?" asked Barrett grumpily. His tree had fallen off the back of the wagon halfway from the orchard, and he'd jumped off to retrieve it. But the driver hadn't noticed, and Barrett had had to walk all the way back, dragging his tree behind him.

"That Al's in love."

Barrett scrunched up his face. "What the hell? *You*? Now you're in *love*?"

"No," said Alex, punching Fitz in the arm. "I'm *not* in love. I wouldn't even know . . . No. I'm not."

Fitz stared at Alex knowingly, and Alex glared back at him, turning back to Barrett. "*He's* getting married and having a baby, and he suddenly sees the whole world through his own special love-colored glasses."

Barrett raised his eyebrows at Fitz. "By the way, it's crazy that you're having a baby."

"Finally someone's making sense," said Alex.

"It's good crazy," said Fitz, looking over at Daisy. "It's crazy awesome."

"It doesn't freak you out?" asked Alex.

Fitz shrugged. "I want to be a good husband to Daisy. I want to be a good father to our baby. But freaked-out? Nah. I've wanted this for so long, you wouldn't believe it."

"And you?" asked Alex, looking beyond Fitz to Barrett. "*You* ready to get married? Ready to give up the boardroom?"

"To Emily? Yeah. Tomorrow. And I'm not giving up anything, Al. I'm still going to do killer deals. They'll be even better because she's amazing at sorting through strategy. The Harrison–Lowry merger? To be honest, that was more Emily than me."

"Speaking of Harrison," said Fitz, turning to Barrett. "I noticed you trying to strong-arm Chris Winslow into going to Devon in January."

"Someone's got to go. For at least a few months, to oversee things," said Barrett, sighing as they moved up in line again, dragging their trees behind them. "You can't go. You're having a baby. And I can't go. I'm getting married."

"Chris isn't interested?" asked Alex.

Barrett shook his head. "He said he would if there was no other option, but he'd prefer to stay in Philly. And it doesn't make sense for Cam to go. He's the money guy, like you."

"We need to ask Stratton," said Fitz, grimacing.

Although Stratton was an excellent project manager, his people skills sometimes left something to be desired, which didn't make him an ideal choice. Barrett groaned.

"Maybe we could get him some coaching?" suggested Alex. "Before he goes?"

"I don't think it would help," said Fitz. "It's the way he blurts things out. Especially when he has to work with women."

Barrett nodded, then shrugged. "We don't have a choice. I think it's got to be Strat . . . unless *you* want to talk to Christopher about it?"

Alex's eyes widened. "I don't think I'm very popular with the Winslows right now."

"Business is business," insisted Barrett, "and you know Chris better than me or Fitz."

"Fine," grumbled Alex. "I'll talk to Chris."

"Speaking of the Winslows," said Barrett, flicking his chin at Jessie before continuing, "you two look good together. You don't look much like *friends*, but you look . . . I don't know . . . happy. Like she actually means something to you. Like you might let her stick around beyond Sunday brunch."

"Shut up, Barrett," said Alex, but his face softened as he glanced over at Jessie and caught her emerald eyes. She grinned, hopping off the wagon and walking over to him with a good bit of sass in her stride.

"Excuse me, sir," said Jessie, when she was within a few feet of him. "Were you just checking me out?"

"Huh?"

She put her hands on her slim hips. "I was sitting over there with my friends, and I'm pretty sure I noticed . . . you. Checking me. Out."

Alex heard Fitz and Barrett laughing softly behind him, and he grinned at Jessie. "What if I was?"

She took a step closer to him. "You should know that I have a boyfriend."

"Oh, really?"

"Mm-hm," she said, taking one more step.

"Lucky guy," said Alex, dropping his glance, losing himself in those mind-blowing, soft, red lips.

"Lucky me," she said, so close to him now that he could smell tea roses, he could see the lusty darkness in her eyes, he could feel the heat she was throwing off her body. She leaned a little bit closer, and in front of Barrett, Fitz, Emily, and Daisy, she entwined her arms around his neck and kissed him.

And Alex English, who never dated any girl more than thrice and who swore he'd never have another girlfriend again, dropped his tree, pulled his girlfriend, Jessie, into his arms, and kissed her back.

Chapter 8

Jessie wasn't nervous.

At least that's what she told herself as she and Alex pulled out of the driveway of Haverford Park and headed back into the city to have dinner at Alex's apartment. The Christmas tree farm had been tons of fun, and Jessie had greatly enjoyed getting to know Emily and Daisy a little bit better, but mostly she loved being with Alex.

Since their talk against the hedges at Westerly that morning, it seemed like Alex had stopped fighting his feelings for her. All day he had reached for her easily in front of his family. And when he wasn't touching her—holding her hand, putting his arm around her waist, or kissing her in the tree-baling line—he watched her, his eyes heavy-lidded and deliberate, scorching her skin with the heat of his gaze. She'd said she wanted a man who couldn't take his eyes off her, right? Well, Alex was certainly delivering.

Jessie felt it in her bones, in her head, and in her heart: a barrier that was between them had fallen, which meant that anything could happen tonight. Except, now that the opportunity was presenting itself, in an exasperating turn of events, Jessie wasn't sure if she was ready.

"You okay?" Alex asked as he turned onto the highway, the dying sun shining orange and lavender in the rearview mirror as they raced toward his apartment. "You're sort of quiet."

"I'm fine," she said. "It was such a nice day."

"Barrett and Fitz gave me a little bit of a hard time about you."

She shifted in her seat to face him. "About me? Why? They don't approve?"

"They totally approve. I think they're in shock. All four of them, in fact."

"Daisy and Emily may have mentioned you don't bring dates to family events very often."

"Ever, Jess. I don't *ever* bring dates to family events. Occasionally I'll schedule a date for a gala or benefit. Otherwise, I play the field." He cleared his throat. "Except for . . . now. With you."

"It could go to a girl's head," she teased, but her heart fluttered, both from what he was saying and the idea that they were about to spend an evening completely alone as an exclusive couple.

She was excited to have him all to herself, but all those women whom she swore didn't bother her? As they got closer and closer to Alex's apartment, where so many had availed themselves of his gorgeous body, she couldn't help it. Doubts encroached.

"What's going on in *this* girl's head?" he asked.

"Nothing," she answered a little too quickly.

"I know women, Jess. I know when they're overthinking something, and—I say this without a shred of arrogance—I also know when they're overthinking me."

"You know your history doesn't bother me, right? The women?"

He clenched his jaw. "So you say."

"And it really doesn't. But I'm—" She licked her lips and pressed them together. "I mean, I've had boyfriends, of

course, and lovers, but nothing like . . . I mean, my expe-
rience isn't . . ." Her face flamed with heat, and she sighed
loudly, looking out the window.

To her surprise, Alex pulled into the parking lot of an
abandoned gas station in the Philadelphia city limits and
put the car in park, turning to face her.

"You're worried . . ."

She nodded.

". . . about the others." His voice was level, but his eyes
searched hers hard.

"I can't compete," she confessed, and her voice was so soft,
she almost couldn't hear the words in her own ears.

"Jess," he whispered slowly, shaking his head back and
forth as his face softened and saddened before her. "You've
got it backwards. *They* can't compete. Not one of them. In
fact, I don't have one memory with another woman that
competes with this moment, right here, right now."

"Oh," she gasped, surprised when tears brightened her
eyes.

He twisted his body to face hers, reaching out to cup her
cheek and swipe away a tear with his thumb. "Not one of
them really knew me. Not one of them ever looked at me
with trust. Not one of them ever sideswiped my heart. It
was just sex. Fun, but ultimately meaningless. And I don't
know if that comforts you or disgusts you, but don't ever
worry that my mind will wander to someone else when I'm
with you. All you see is me? Jess, you have to know . . . all I
see is you."

Jessie's cheeks were wet with tears by the time Alex finished in a soft, reverent voice, and she swiftly unbuckled her
seat belt and reached for him. Their lips collided with hunger and reassurance, with wonder and want, and something
deeper that neither of them was quite ready to name. Jessie
whimpered as his tongue slipped into her mouth, struggling

to get closer to him, but impeded by the console between them. She fisted her hands in his shirt, her blood on fire for him, wanting nothing more than to rip off his clothes and rip off hers and let him drag her into the backseat to prove that all he could see . . . was her.

Her chest heaved with short, ragged pants when she pulled away from him abruptly, hurtling herself back into her seat with the frustration of unquenched desire.

"How much longer till we get to your apartment?" she panted, staring out the windshield.

Alex burned rubber pulling out of that abandoned gas station, driving like the devil was at his heels, or like heaven was just around the next bend.

God, she burned hot.

Whatever chivalry Alex was trying to exercise was dying a swift death, burned to ashes by the heat Jessie was bringing to the equation. Think of another woman? It was impossible when he was with her. Aside from the fact that she actually meant something to him—something more real and important with every moment they spent together—Jessie, for all that she was younger and less experienced than Alex, was not shy. She wasn't some shrinking violet who gasped every time he hurled a hot glance her way.

From the beginning, she had met him on his own ground, suggestive, demanding, wanting, taking. Alex was famous for his high libido, and in a perfect twist of fate, Jessie seemed to lust for him with the same appetite and passion that Alex did for her.

Taking all of her, thrusting up into her wet heat, was such a heady and imminent fantasy, the semihardness that had started when she'd kissed him wouldn't subside. As he pulled into his parking space in the basement garage of his building, he reminded himself that, while she'd mentioned something this morning about staying over and their heat seemed to be off the charts, he should temper his expectations. Whatever happened between them would be at her pace and hers alone.

As the sounds of the engine all but disappeared, they sat in quiet darkness, neither of them saying anything or reaching for the other, just staring straight ahead at the dark concrete wall of the parking garage, the mutual shallowness of their breathing the only indication of how much their bodies were trying to stay in control.

"It was nice of Fitz to offer to bring over the tree to your place tomorrow," said Jessie, casting a glance at him.

"Yeah," said Alex, wetting his lips and wishing his body would cool it. They hadn't even had dinner yet, but damn it, he'd never wanted a girl—never, not ever—as much as he wanted Jessie. "So, um . . ."

Without turning to him, her left hand landed on his arm.

"Alex," she said. "Do you know what's going to happen tonight?"

He swallowed. God, she tied him in knots with the way she walked the line between bold and sweet. It made him uncertain, like he was all new at this, and because it was her, Jessie, he liked it. He liked the feeling that he couldn't predict every move, every sigh, every look. It made him breathless with anticipation in a way he couldn't ever remember feeling before. Jesus, it was exciting.

"Nope."

"Me neither."

Her fingers curled gently into his arm, and when he looked over at her, her breasts rose and fell swiftly.

"You know what I *do* know?" he asked her.

"Tell me," she whispered, still not looking at him.

"You're calling the shots. Whatever happens tonight? It's all you, Jessie-girl. You tell me what you want, and I say yes. That's how it's going to be with you and me."

"How do you know you'll want what I want?"

"I just do. Plus, I'm not saying no to you anymore. I want—no, I *have* to give you whatever you want. I *need* to."

"If it's all about me, what about you?"

"I'm a guy, Jessie, and you're the most gorgeous woman I've ever seen. And I've had feelings for you since I was a kid. I'm not going to lie; I want you bad. But even more than that, I want you to feel safe with me, and comfortable, and . . . good. I want to make you feel good, Jess, because that's all I feel when I'm with you. I feel good. I feel . . . like I'm not some filthy piece of philandering shit." He covered her hand with his to soften the blunt ugliness of his words. His voice was gentle. "I have no expectations. Whatever you want, it's yours."

She turned to face him, and in the dim light afforded by the pale orange lights of the underground garage, he could see the softness, the tenderness, the reach-into-his-chest-and-squeeze-his-heart trust looking back at him.

And that's when Alex English realized it: Margaret had been right, and damn it, Fitz had been right too. He wasn't sure how it had happened so quickly, but he had fallen in love with Jessica Winslow.

Jessie watched his eyes widen, heard the soft, surprised gasp escape his lips as his eyes locked with hers and held on. He'd been so confident during his little speech, and then she'd lifted her eyes to him . . . and she saw it: he truly, deeply cared for her. He might even—

No, she thought. *Don't go there. Five weeks of fun. That's all you agreed to. You can't change the rules now.*

She swallowed, forcing herself to look away from him, because the hammering of her heart was almost painful. "Let's go upstairs."

Detaching his hand from hers, he circled the car, opened her door, and held out his hand again. He pulled her toward the glass door that led to a simple vestibule with an elevator, then put his key in the elevator door and it opened.

"Hey," he said, as they entered the small space together. "I never asked what you wanted for dinner."

You, she thought, her cheeks flushing at the thought.

He still held her hand, and she concentrated on the soft warmth of his fingers laced through hers, the way nothing had ever felt as perfect as her hand in Alex's. Would it feel that perfect when their bodies were joined together too? Would she fit him like a glove? Like something that was built especially for him? Would she be able to quell her nerves enough to make it to that moment tonight? Would he?

She hazarded a glance up at him.

He looked cool and confident. The straight, strong curve of his jaw tilted at an angle as he watched the numbers slowly go up. Internally, Jessie shook her head at her foolishness. She highly doubted Alex English ever met a bedroom or a naked woman who made him nervous.

He caught her eye, raising his eyebrows, a small smile playing at the corners of his gorgeous lips. "Dinner?"

"Anything," she answered, wishing her heart would stop its fierce pounding.

"You want to order or should I cook?"

This distracted her. "You cook?"

"Oh, yeah," he boasted, his eyes twinkling. "All of us do."

"The English brothers cook?"

He grinned, nodding at her. "Yep. My mother insisted. Susannah taught all of us the basics. Scrambled eggs, garden salad, marinated chicken breasts—"

Her laugh interrupted him. "I don't know why it's so difficult for me to picture this."

"Oh, I'll help you," he said, as the elevator dinged to tell them it had arrived at his floor. Alex held the door open for her, gesturing to the left.

She stepped out, and he grabbed her hand again as they walked down a long carpeted hallway that reminded her of a corridor you'd find in a very elegant hotel (which did nothing to calm her nerves).

Gold-framed mirrors and botanical pictures were hung on the walls, and every twenty feet or so, they passed an apartment door. Jessie couldn't help wondering exactly how many other women had made this walk with Alex, holding his hand, glancing at the same pictures, checking their reflections surreptitiously in the mirrors, as they got closer and closer.

"Picture five boys in white aprons standing at that metal island in the center of my parents' kitchen at Haverford. Susannah stood on the other side, bowls and bread and eggs and vegetables between us. And my mother sternly watched from the corner, smoking a cigarette, assuring the absence of any shenanigans. Barrett was fourteen that summer, so Fitz was twelve, I was eleven, Strat was eight, and Wes was six."

Jessie grinned, able to picture all of them perfectly.

"And little Jessie Winslow was five," he added softly, stopping at a dark wood door that had a brass knocker under the number five. He pointed to the five and winked at her.

She laughed softly, grateful for the way the conversation was relaxing her.

As Alex dropped her hand to unlock the door, Jessie pictured herself at five years old. Her mother would braid her long, black hair every morning into a tight French braid that started at her crown and ended halfway down her back.

"Better for riding, playing, and mischief," her mother would add with a grin before encouraging her to go find Christopher at the stables or ask the Story girls to come over for a swim.

With the old sorrow that never really goes away, Jessie also recalled that her father was still alive when she was five, tall and strong, so big, she thought he was indomitable, maybe even immortal. She'd been wrong.

Alex's palm gently caressing her face made her lift watery eyes. She smiled at him. "When I was five, my dad was still alive."

Alex nodded, his face tender and searching. "I remember him."

"Do you?" she asked hopefully, leaning toward him.

"Mm-hm. He was big, and he had jet-black hair like yours." Alex reached for a long strand of dark hair and wound it around his finger. "And a black mustache."

"He did," said Jessie, still smiling, still on the brink of tears.

No one in London had ever known her father, and her brothers—their mother's sons through and through—had adopted a stiff-upper-lip mentality about his loss. They rarely talked about him, and though Jessie had quietly accepted that remembrances weren't the Winslow way, she couldn't help that she *wanted* to remember.

And here was Alex, giving her that chance.

It didn't surprise Jessie that Alex should offer her this safe haven, this gentle space, where she could unwrap her memories. He was the same Alex who had been kind when she was so little, so sad, so desperately in need of someone to make her feel special and wanted. What Alex offered now was the same sanctuary he'd offered when she was a child, and it was achingly familiar. So, no, it didn't surprise her, but, oh God, how it seized and claimed something at the very depths of her being, confirming what she'd always known. This beautiful man, who traded in debauchery, was her inmost desire, the unlikely home of her heart.

"He played Santa," said Alex. "Do you remember that?"

She nodded, biting her lower lip.

"Yeah. Your mom would put white shoe polish or something on his mustache, but it would sort of flake off as the kids climbed on his lap at the Westerly Christmas party."

"That's why the little kids always went first," she said, a tear snaking its way down her cheek.

Alex swiped it away, resting on her smile for a moment before continuing. He understood. Somehow he understood that her tears didn't mean "stop"—they meant "keep going."

"He and my dad would smoke cigars on the terrace sometimes on a summer evening."

"My mother hated it."

"So did mine," said Alex. "She'd say that Taylor Winslow was a bad influence." He chuckled softly, but his smile faded. "Oh, sorry, Jess. She felt bad about that, I think. After he died."

"He *was* a bad influence," said Jessie, as she beamed at Alex through tears. "He was always sneaking us sweets after we'd brushed our teeth. Letting us stay up late to watch horror movies while my mother played bridge at the club."

"He had that booming laugh," said Alex. "Scared me a little when I was small."

"I loved it," said Jessie. "If I think hard, I can still hear it."

"Me too," said Alex, palming her face gently and using his thumbs to wipe away her tears. "It's good to remember."

"Thank you, Alex," she said softly, and he pulled her into his arms, wrapping them around her as she swallowed the lump in her throat. His hands rubbed her back slowly, and Jessie breathed deeply, memorizing the smell of Polo Black and pine and fresh country air mixed with leather and cotton. She rested her cheek on Alex's chest, allowing him to comfort her in the darkened doorway of his apartment. The swelling of her heart told her what she already knew, what she'd known for years, what she'd *always* known.

She was desperately in love with Alex English.

Then. Now. Forever.

To prove that Susannah's training hadn't been in vain, Alex decided to whip up the prettiest little omelets he could manage with the slim pickings in his bachelor's fridge. Grimacing as he checked out the questionable contents, he had no choice but to make do with some week-old Gouda that needed to be scraped a little, an onion, and tarragon flakes. As Jessie walked around his apartment tentatively, Alex kept an eye on her from the kitchen.

Her arms were crossed almost defensively, one hand holding the stem of a wineglass close to her chest. She stared at the slick black leather couch, black lacquered coffee table, sideboard, and bookcases. She looked down at the plush cream area rug that covered the space between the couch and fireplace, carefully stepping around it.

He knew what she was thinking—she'd been thinking it in the car and again in the hallway before he'd distracted her with stories of childhood cooking lessons. She was thinking about the other women—the multitude of others who had come before. He could feel it, and he hated it. But while his life before Jessie was indefensible, he also couldn't change it, and despite his ample warnings, she seemed dead set on spending time with him. His mind cautioned softly that it couldn't possibly be that simple—she couldn't just accept her place in the middle of hundreds of other women—but

Alex wanted her so badly, felt so grateful for the absence of that terrible ache that had plagued him for weeks. It was Jessie who somehow soothed his soul, who focused his attention on one perfect woman, who made playing the field temporarily obsolete. If she offered herself to him, even for the wistful space of four weeks, he didn't have the strength or will to turn her away.

He cracked four eggs and added a little Parmalat, mixing with a whisk just as Susannah had shown them all so long ago. Jessie stopped in front of his modern fireplace, checking out the framed painting over the mantel.

It was a new acquisition. He'd called his decorator a few days ago and had the old one—an ancient Chinese rice paper print of two people fucking—swapped out for a modern piece. It had been an easy choice of the paintings offered. Shades of green fought for dominion on the canvas, but emerald won. The green was the exact shade of Jessie's eyes, and as soon as Alex had seen a photo of the painting over e-mail, he asked for it to be framed, shipped, and hung by Thanksgiving. No small feat, but with the right resources, not impossible either.

After a long moment, Jessie turned to him. Her forehead was furrowed, and her lips were soft but closed in an expression at once curious and confused. She gestured to the painting.

"This is a Lila Leighton."

"Mm-hm," he said, placing an onion on a cutting board.

"An original."

"As far as I know."

She looked up at the painting again. "Lila Leighton's work just hit the Astraea Gallery in Manhattan eight days ago."

"Oh?"

"Yes. Which means you bought that painting this week." Her eyes cut to his from across the room. "But it's an especially odd choice for you . . . since, as of Tuesday, you didn't get modern art."

He shrugged, his cheeks flushing as he bent down to grab a frying pan from under the oven. When he straightened, she had crossed the room and stood before him.

"Alex, why did you buy that painting?" she asked softly, searching his eyes.

Helpless. He flicked his glance to the splotches of emerald green in the heart of the painting, then back to her. The truth tumbled from his lips without permission. "The green is the same color as your eyes."

"You bought a *Lila Leighton* because of a shade of green?"

"It's the only shade of green that matters," he explained.

She nodded, clenching her jaw, her expression inscrutable. He wished he knew what was going on in her head. Was she freaked-out that she'd mentioned an interest in modern art and he'd purchased an expensive piece, sight unseen, later that day?

Jessie still had her coat on, her arms crossed over her chest, and suddenly Alex realized that part of the reason he'd purchased the painting was because, if she ever came to his apartment, he wanted her to feel at home. He wanted something in *his* space to belong to *her.*

Placing the frying pan on the stovetop and the whisked eggs in the fridge, he reached forward, tugging the wineglass from her fingers and setting it on the counter next to the cutting board. He put his hands gently on her forearms and pulled her arms away from her body. Holding her eyes, he slid her purse down her arm and placed it beside her wine. Carefully, he unbuttoned the black buttons of her coat and slid it down her shoulders, draping it over one of the kitchen chairs pushed into the table behind him.

"I bought it for you," he whispered, baring his soul to her, hoping that she would see how much he wanted to be worthy of her, how much he wanted her in his world for however long she was willing to stay.

She clenched her jaw again and nodded, like she'd already known. Her eyes were heavy as they captured his.

"I'm going to fall in love with you, Alex," she murmured. "I'm sorry. I know that wasn't the deal."

And then he understood why she'd looked so stricken ever since she'd seen the painting—not because she was freaked-out or upset with him, but because of her feelings for him. It was staggering how deeply her admission affected him. For a moment—just a millisecond of a moment—his heart stopped beating. It stopped because it had to physically break free of the past before starting again. And when it did, it beat for her. Only for her.

Alex read her wide eyes and grim expression perfectly. She was waiting to see what would happen next. She was giving him the chance to walk away, right here and now. She was telling him that if he had a problem with her loving him, now was the moment to say so.

His eyes swept across her face, caressing it with his gaze, the tenderness he felt for her infused into his glance. He couldn't say anything. He could only stare back at a face so lovely, so pure and beautiful, it made his chest full, it made his heart whole, it made him ache with a longing he'd never known. This girl—this rare, exceptional woman—made him, Alex English, the manwhore, the Casanova, the womanizing playboy . . . *helpless.*

So goddamned helpless.

He didn't walk away.

He stepped forward.

Cupping her face with his hands, he lowered his head, dropping his lips to hers, which opened like petals, welcoming him into the sweet, wet heaven of her mouth with a surprised, relieved sigh. His tongue found hers, swirling

Katy Regnery

around it, deepening the kiss as his hands skimmed down her cheeks, over the throbbing pulse in her throat, and down her back. Her arms looped around his neck, pulling him closer as she arched against his chest. Slipping his hands under the velvety texture of her sweater, he found a different softness altogether. The skin of her back was smooth and warm, and as he flattened his palms on the even plains, she whimpered, leaning into him to tell him she wanted more.

Holding her tight and refusing to surrender her lips, he maneuvered her to his kitchen table, slipping his hands to her hips and lifting her. She widened her legs, beckoning him closer, welcoming him into her space. As he stepped between them, her hands reached for his hips, pulling the shirt from the waist of his jeans, her fingers finding the warm, taut skin beneath as she pulled him as close as possible. His hands skated up her back again, finding the clasp of her bra and expertly unlatching it. Alex splayed his hands on the unobstructed skin of her back, dropping his lips to her throat as she arched against him again.

"Jessie, Jessie, Jessie-girl, I want you so bad," he murmured against her pulse, which raced and pleaded against the sensitive skin of her lips. He drew the heels of his hands forward until they pressed against the sides of her breasts, the softness so close and so enticing, he didn't know how he was managing to move so slowly.

And then he did know. He knew exactly.

This wasn't a one-night thing. There was no rush. There was urgency, but instead of pushing things along as quickly as he usually did, he wanted to draw out every touch, every sigh, every murmur. He wanted to record all of it and save it in some corner of his heart earmarked for Jessie. Later, when she was gone, if he could bear it, he'd be able to revisit the memory of what it felt like to be with her, to be with someone he loved for the first time in his life.

Jessie moaned as his fingers tilted up like a fan, each digit brushing her sensitive nipples in turn until his fingers splayed perfectly over the hot, heaving flesh of her breasts.

"Alex," she whimpered, shimmying forward on the table to press her pelvis against his, surging forward into him as she leaned her forehead on his chest in surrender.

His erection strained uncomfortably against his jeans as he pressed up against her, dipping his head to take her lower lip between his. At the same time he squeezed her nipples between his fingers, eliciting a louder whimper from Jessie. She grabbed his lip with her teeth and curled her fingers into his hips. He gasped from the sensation of her nails biting into his skin and thrust his tongue into her mouth, rolling one nipple between his thumb and forefinger as he cupped her other breast in the palm of his hand.

If she didn't still have her sweater on, he would have dropped his lips to that pebble of flesh and sucked it into his mouth until she writhed against him, begged him to stop, and pleaded with him for more. And he knew she would. The rising heat between them was white-hot and so intense, his breathing became ragged as he imagined them in his bed together.

As if reading his mind, her fingers released his hips and reached for the hem of her sweater, pushing it up over her belly, over her breasts, baring them to him.

Alex drew back, looking into her eyes as he pulled the sweater and bra quickly over her head. Her fingers trembled as they worked on the buttons of his shirt, finally opening it and dragging it down over his shoulders. He reached behind his neck and yanked his undershirt over his head, baring his chest to her as she had to him. But before reaching for her, he flattened his palms on the table on either side of her hips, exercising a level of self-control he didn't know he had. He wouldn't even drop his eyes to her breasts until she gave him permission.

"Tell me," he growled softly, holding her green eyes hostage with his.

"I want you to touch me," she whispered.

"How?" he demanded.

Her eyes were obsidian pools as she stared back at him. She slipped her trembling fingers to her chest, trailing them between her breasts, where they rested. "Here." Then she moved them again, over the soft skin of her tummy, underneath her panties. "And here."

His breath caught and his eyes fluttered for a moment, drunk with the carte blanche she was giving him, before his blood surged, hot and demanding, as untapped wells of desire rose to flood his senses. He'd never known want like this, never truly known what it would feel like to marry passion with love. Now that he knew, he didn't know how he would ever return to his old life again. Whatever came after Jessie would never be able to chase the high of having her. At the same time she was offering him unforeseen heights of pleasure, she was destroying everything he'd ever known.

And yet.

All he wanted—in the entire world—was to pleasure her. "Done."

Letting his hands smooth up the sides of her hips, he held her in place as he dropped his lips to her shoulder, skimming them along the delicate curve that led to her throat. She trailed her fingers up his back lightly with a touch that made him shiver as his hands skated from her hips to her waist.

His lips dropped lower to the miracle that was the base of her neck, licking, nipping, resting, as her fingers continued their ascent, following the line of his spine to his collarbones, where they split, discovering the hard outline of his form with the feather touch of her fingers.

His lips descended still lower, to the smooth planes of her chest under her neck, the lightly freckled skin smooth and even under his unworthy lips, which brushed, gently dusting, seeking, daring to move lower with every deep breath she took.

Her fingers found their destination in the soft, short, curled hair on the back of his neck, as her palms cradled the soft skin behind his ears. And his hands found their journey's end at the same time, cupping the fullness of her breasts as his lips found their own heaven, sucking one of her waiting nipples into the hot wetness of his mouth.

"Alex!" she gasped, arching her back as his teeth grazed the taut, delicate skin.

As he gently loved one hard bud with his tongue, his thumb brushed slow, deliberate circles around its twin. And then his lips shifted, loving the second nipple as he had the first, his thumb and forefinger rolling its slickened mate until a cry rent from the back of her throat.

Her ankles had locked around his back, and her fingers curled into his scalp as she yanked his head up roughly to slam her mouth into his, swallowing his deep groan as they feverishly collided, their tongues delving into each other's mouths to taste and touch, furiously seeking relief from the growing hunger between them.

Reckless and impatient, they were being swept away by their feelings, so how Alex managed to swim to the surface of reason for one last moment, he'd never know. He pulled away from her abruptly, needing to be sure of exactly where they were going.

"What do you want?" he demanded, his voice strained and breathless as he reached up, almost roughly, to clasp her face.

Her tongue slipped out to wet her lips.

"You. Your bed. Now," she said between panted breaths.

His self-control was almost gone. But this wasn't just some random woman. It was Jessie. Her words scorched a path from her mouth to his heart, then even lower, where he throbbed in readiness for her.

"Jess," he groaned. "*Please* be sure. Once we start, I don't know if I'll be able to stop."

"I'm sure. I want you, Alex," she whispered. "I always have."

Completely helpless.

Because he wanted her just as much as she wanted him. Because he needed her laid out on his bed, her black hair on his white pillow, her body soft and wet and willing beneath his. Because here, now, tonight, with this extraordinary woman who made him feel things he'd never thought he would feel, everything he'd thought he needed and wanted in his life slipped away, until all that was left was Jessica Winslow. All he needed and wanted . . . was her.

Tucking his hands under her backside, he lifted her off the table, her ankles still locked around his back. Without surrendering her lips, he carried her through the darkness of his apartment, through the living room, down a hallway, kicking open his bedroom door, and not stopping until he was sitting on the edge of his bed with the half-naked girl of his dreams still wrapped around him like the miracle he never saw coming.

Chapter 9

Jessie had never experienced anything close to the sheer and desperate longing she felt to give herself—completely, entirely, without reservation—to Alex.

Her whole body hummed with need for him, with awareness, with the promise of what was coming next. Straddling his lap, she urged her hips forward, rolling over the enormous bulge straining against his jeans. Her breasts, sensitive and throbbing from his earlier attention, rubbed against the hard smoothness of his ripped chest, making her gasp with pleasure as he ran his hands through her hair, pulling her lips to his.

His mouth was more demanding than it had been in the kitchen, but her eager tongue met his measure for measure, stroke for stroke. Her hands dropped to his pecs, flattening before trailing along the ridges of muscle that rippled and flexed under her fingertips. She edged back slightly so she could unbutton his jeans, which opened with a pop, but before she could reach for his zipper, he surprised her by grabbing her wrists and looping them back around his neck. Sliding his fingers down her back, he stopped at her ass, which he cupped in his strong hands, forcing her legs wider as he thrust up against her.

Jessie moaned, partly because her body was responding to Alex in ways she'd never felt before, but also because her frustration was mounting. She liked foreplay as much as the next girl, but for the first time in her life, the destination felt more important, more crucial, more necessary than the journey. She sensed he was purposely moving slow, but what Jessie really wanted was to do the deed. She felt urgent, somewhat because she was still worried about how she'd rank among the multitudes, to get it over with.

Teasing the hairs on the back of Alex's neck and loving the way he shivered lightly, she arched her back again, pushing her breasts into his chest before clasping his head between her hands and forcing his neck to bend. Submitting to her request, Alex scorched a trail from her mouth, down her chin, over the throbbing pulse in her neck, to her chest, finally drawing one of her rock-hard nipples into his mouth. His cheeks caved in as he sucked her to the edge of pain, releasing the bud with a loud *pop* before shifting to the other. Jessie panted, writhed against him, whimpered from the sharpness of the pleasure, and curled her nails reflexively into his scalp.

"Alexxx . . . ," she moaned, bowing away from his mouth, leaning against his arms as his lips trailed down over her tummy.

He tilted his face so that his jaw caressed the skin of her belly. His voice was thick and low as he murmured, "I want to taste you, Jess. I want to feel you come against my mouth."

"Oh God." She sighed, goose bumps lighting across her skin from the rawness in his voice. "*Please*, Alex."

The arm around her back pushed her forward, and he slid his hands under her arms to pull her from his lap. He lay her gently on the bed with her legs hanging over the end. His fingers worked quickly to release the button of her jeans and unzip them with a quiet whoosh. Jessie lifted her hips, feeling the already-liquid heat of her sex quiver with anticipation of Alex's mouth touching her so intimately.

"Jesus, Jessica, you're beautiful," he breathed, staring at her almost-naked body in the moonlight while pulling off her boots and jeans. She leaned up on her elbows and caught his eyes, dark and languid with tenderness and hunger. He dropped them to the white satin panties that stood between him and the throbbing skin underneath that ached for his touch. Flattening his hand over the slick material, she heard him inhale sharply. His eyes cut to hers again, and he licked his lips.

"You're wet. You're so ready for me," he said, his voice thick and low, and a little awed.

"I am," she whimpered. "We could just . . ."

"No," Alex insisted. "No, Jess, I'm not rushing this. Not with you. I'm going to make you come half a dozen different ways before tonight is over. I promise you that, baby. But first I'm going to kneel in front of you and love your clit with my tongue until you scream my name so loud, the entire city of Philadelphia knows Alex English is off the market until Christmas." He paused. "Got it?"

Jessie had stopped breathing halfway through his words, but now she gasped for a breath, nodding and throwing her arm over her eyes as he laughed softly. His fingers slipped into the waistband of her underwear, and he pulled them slowly and deliberately down her long legs. Placing those long legs gently on his shoulders, he knelt on the floor at the foot of the bed and leaned forward, sliding his hands to her hips, which he pulled, slowly, gently, toward him, to the very edge of the bed.

Her breathing was so shallow, it was making her dizzy. As though he knew, Alex rested his forehead on the smooth skin right above the trim triangle of curly hair at the junction of her thighs, and his hands skimmed her hips and waist, coming to rest, flat and heavy, atop her rib cage.

"Breathe, Jess," he whispered, the heat of his breath caressing the most intimate parts of her body as the weight of his hands pressed down gently under her breasts. "Just breathe."

He flipped one hand over, smoothing the backs of fingers along the ridges of her ribs, and Jess obeyed his command, taking a deep breath and relaxing, bowing her back slightly and closing her eyes.

The same hand slid to her waist, then slipped lower to graze the skin of her hip. He lifted his head from her belly and pressed his hand, flush and firm, over her curls. She whimpered again, awaiting his touch. His fingers moved like a whisper over her sensitive flesh, delving into her hidden valley and parting her with the V of his fingers. And suddenly his lips landed on the softest, most delicate tissue of her body, and her fingers fisted in his bedspread as her hips lifted off the mattress. His tongue brushed slowly back and forth across her clitoris, and she whimpered and panted, the sensations teasing and agonizing every time he made contact with the rigid bud of nerves, before sweeping to the side again. Just when she started to anticipate his movements, his tongue switched course. Moving in a clockwise motion, he circled her clit again and again as the hand resting on her ribs slid down, over her belly, holding the outside of her thigh gently before reaching up between her legs. He inserted two fingers inside her body and Jess gasped, then moaned loudly, bringing her knuckle to her mouth to bite, to keep from thrusting her hips into his face.

The pressure in her belly mounted as his fingers pressed against the inside wall of her sex. "So, sweet, Jessie-girl. So sweet," he murmured, and the buzz of his deep voice against her skin made the building heat thicken and boil, her inner muscles gathering and tensing as she felt his lips pucker and softly kiss her clit as he had her tongue.

Her breathing became more frantic and erratic as her skin flushed hot, then cold. Her hips lifted rhythmically against him, the delicious, terrifying, incomparable pressure swirling now, building higher and higher, as she pressed her head back against his mattress and her eyes rolled back in her head.

When she felt the gentle, forbidden graze of his teeth against the sensitive folds, her body clenched, rigid and straining. She held her breath for just a moment, struggling and coiled, before screaming his name. Her body exploded. Waves of pleasure made her inner muscles writhe and pulse around his fingers as she bucked and jerked against his tongue, which lapped and licked her soft skin until her tremors began to subside.

She was jelly. She was half-dead. She barely felt him move, but heard the quiet *zzzz* of his zipper and the rustle of his jeans hitting the floor. His weight sunk the mattress beside her, and he folded her into the naked heaven of his arms.

She felt his breath on her face, smelled the sweet saltiness of her come on his lips. He leaned forward and kissed her forehead, then brushed his lips over her closed eyelids before drawing her as close as possible and lowering his cheek to the pillow beside her.

And Jessica, who was madly in love, whose body felt like it had been adored to the point of worship, savored the contact of him pressed flush and naked against her, deceiving herself—for just a moment—that unlike the others, he belonged to her and she belonged to him. But the moment passed as her throbbing body calmed, and she was left with the aching pain that came from acknowledging the sad and terrible truth:

Belonging to Alex was only temporary.

For the first time that Alex could ever remember, instead of seeking instant gratification from his partner, he paused.

He waited for her. Little by little her breathing slowed to normal, though aftershocks made her shiver and tremble in his arms as she came down from her high. She took a deep, shaky breath as her lashes fluttered before opening. Her eyes, dilated and black in the dim light, instantly found his staring back at her.

"Alex," she whispered in a broken voice.

As he looked closer, he noticed the tears brightening her eyes. Smoothing a hand over her back, he leaned forward to kiss her gently. "Are you okay?"

"*Where do I go now?*" she asked in a quiet, devastated sob.

"You don't go anywhere. You stay with me," he said softly, not totally understanding her meaning, but sure of his answer all the same.

She swallowed, her breath still ragged and shallow as she gazed back at him. "I've never . . . I mean, I've never felt—"

"Neither have I," he said, interrupting her before she could finish.

Alex knew what he felt, and he was pretty sure she felt the same, but he simply wasn't ready to hear it or say it, and he hoped that was okay.

She managed a small smile for him, but he could see it didn't go all the way to her eyes, and that bothered him.

"Are you okay?" he asked again.

"Mm-hm."

He searched her face, his fingers kneading the soft skin of her hip as his erection strained between them. It was rock hard and smooth, pressing against her with a hunger that Alex would usually act upon without consideration, but her eyes were sad and worried and more important to him than anything else.

"What do you need?"

Her eyes swam, bleak and frustrated, as she looked up at him. "You."

He nodded, leaning forward to touch his lips to hers as she rolled to her back. Pulling his arm from under her, he rolled with her, settling the weight of his body on top of hers and kissing her gently with deep, sensual strokes of his tongue. She tore her mouth from his, and her hands slid down his back, fingers curling into his ass.

She looked directly into his eyes. "I want you to fuck me. Now."

He flinched at her use of the word *fuck*. He wasn't uncomfortable with the word itself—in fact, he used it near constantly with his other bed partners—but he hated the way it sounded coming out of Jessie's mouth.

He shook his head, staring at her stricken face. Was it possible he had misjudged their growing feelings? Was it possible that like the others she wanted only one thing from him? A torrid night of hot sex and some Sunday morning brunch?

No, his heart protested, clenching at the thought of her possible indifference. *Not her. She cares about you. She told you she was going to fall in love with you.*

"No. Jess, I—"

"Please, Alex. Just do it," she demanded, almost angrily, her nails biting into his skin again.

He rolled off her, panting as he lay on his back, his erection tenting the sheet. He didn't know what was going on, but *fucking* had no place between them. Later maybe, for fun, but not tonight. Not their first time together.

"No," he said softly.

"*Why not*?" she sobbed.

He leaned up on one elbow, looking down at her face, which was covered with wetness. She was crying. God, she was crying.

Alex had no idea what to do. The women who came to his bed were there for one thing. They didn't expect anything of him. They only wanted his body—his tongue, his hands, his lips, his cock. Why was she crying? And what could he say to make her stop?

In the end, he opted for honesty because he didn't know what else to do.

"Because I can't," he whispered gently, tracing the trail of a tear with his fingertip.

"You *can't*? That's what you do! That's who you are!"

He flinched again, from the anger and pain in her voice, from the frustration, from the way, he sensed, she wanted to hurt him a little bit too. But instead of raising his hackles or triggering his flight instinct, her fraught words increased his tenderness and eliminated any urge to retreat. And suddenly the pieces all came together, and he knew what this was about: it was about protecting herself. It was about making sex less than the loving act it could and should and would be between them. It was about keeping it physical to keep herself safe. It was exactly what Alex had done his entire life.

Watching her struggle, his heart surged with love for her, and he palmed her cheek, turning her to face him.

"I can't," he repeated gently but firmly. "That's who I *was*."

Tears poured out of her eyes as she stared back at him.

"That's what I *used* to do. Before you."

She sniffled, taking a deep, ragged breath.

"I'm not going to fuck you, Jess," he said, swiping away a tear with his thumb. "When you're ready, I'm going to make love to you. That's the only way it's going to happen between us. I can't do it another way. Not with you. I won't."

Her eyes fluttered closed, and her neck bent forward in surrender as his hand slid back into her hair. He leaned forward, his lips touching down on hers, tentatively, seeking permission or agreement, waiting in that careful, terrifying silence to see if she'd kiss him back or turn him away.

And Jessica Winslow suddenly stirred to life to take what was hers, pushing him to his back and throwing her leg over his body so that she was straddling him. Her tongue plunged into his mouth, and Alex took it, sucking on it as his heart quickened into a gallop.

Her hands landed on his cheeks as she drew back from him. Her sadness wasn't gone, but he'd managed to soothe it. She offered him a small smile, adding, with breathy certainty, "Then make love to me, Alex."

It was all he needed to hear.

He flipped her over, kneeling between her legs, his blood surging like lava to his groin, which flexed and throbbed for her. Reaching for a condom on his bedside table, he opened the foil envelope with his teeth and sheathed himself quickly, then leaned down to kiss her lips. Sliding his hands under her to pull her closer and tilt her pelvis up, he never dropped her eyes as he inched forward, rubbing the tip of his sex into the folds that he had tasted just a few moments earlier.

Her eyes fluttered closed as she moaned.

"Look at me, Jessica," he demanded.

Her eyes opened again, deep and dark, her mouth open as shallow breaths made her chest rise and fall with urgency. He shifted slightly, drawing back from her, still holding her at an angle.

"Guide me," he whispered, because he wanted her as committed as he was. This wasn't about just taking or just giving. This was about sharing, and he'd have her with love, or he wouldn't have her at all.

With Alex still supporting her, she sat up on his knees, straddling his waist, reaching between their bodies to wrap her hand around his straining flesh.

"Oh, Alex," she murmured, looking at him with surprised eyes, her fingers unable to quite touch as she fisted him.

"It'll be okay."

His breathing was hitched and shallow, her touch doing things to his heart he'd never experienced before. He'd never moved this slowly, this deliberately with anyone, and it was heightening everything about being with her, building up his desire, increasing his passion.

As she tightened her grip experimentally, he winced, clenching his eyes.

"Look at me, Alex," she said softly, an echo of his earlier words.

His eyes flew open, and his lips tilted up in a smile, which made her do the same.

"I told you . . . you couldn't handle me," she said between pants of breath, leaning forward to brush her breasts against his chest as she positioned him at the entrance of her sex. And then—holding his eyes with the boldness he loved so much—she lowered her body down, taking every bit of his length into her waiting heat.

Alex groaned as he surged up and into her, taking what she offered, giving her all of himself. He swelled bigger as the soft, wet ridges of muscle sucked him forward, trembling around him, her breathless cries making him harder.

"Alex," she gasped when he was fully lodged inside of her. "Oh my God."

She arched her back, and he pushed into her again, watching her face as she breathed in sharp, ragged spurts, biting her lip and whimpering sounds of pleasure. Her arms entwined around his neck, and she lifted herself up a little, only to sink down onto him again. He groaned with the sharpest, deepest pleasure he'd ever known, anytime, with anyone.

Leaning forward, he changed their position, urging her down on her back, hovering over her, resting his weight on his elbows. He drew back and thrust forward again, sliding his hands up her sides until he cupped her precious face, dropping his lips to her mouth. He kissed her gently, reverently, refusing to let himself forget—even for a millisecond—who it was beneath him, who was welcoming his undeserving body into hers, who was redeeming a lifetime of debauchery with this single act of love.

And suddenly her question—*Where do I go now?*—made perfect sense to him, because although their arrangement was temporary, any future that didn't include Jess was barely worth imagining. A month with her wasn't enough. A year wouldn't be enough. Nothing would be enough except maybe . . . forever.

Like a slide show, images of her passed through his mind: as a small child, as a young girl, as an older girl leaving for London, who looked into his blue eyes and made him feel special. And suddenly he was watching her turn around and face him in the lobby of her brother's apartment building, training her smile on him and filling his empty heart. She had raised her eyes to his, searching his face with such tenderness and surprise. Every look she gave him, every time she touched him, every gesture telegraphed her trust and . . . yes, her love. For him. For Alex English.

"You love me," he breathed, the words swirling up from the place of light, the place of Jess, in his dark heart. "Don't you?"

His eyes searched hers, and he saw the answer there before she even spoke the word.

"Yes," she sobbed, gasping as he thrust into her again.

Her answer was terrifying and yet somehow so necessary for his very survival, his eyes shuddered closed for a moment in relief and gratitude. The sweetness of knowing how she felt about him made his impending climax, which bore down, huge and imminent, quicken to the point of no return.

Still deeply lodged within her, he shifted to align his pelvis perfectly with hers and slowed his pace, rocking into her slowly, pressing against her clit with every deliberate upward stroke. Her neck arched back, and he felt the almost immediate tightening around him, the way the walls of her sex flexed, the way her breathing changed from ragged to held, the way her head pressed urgently into the pillow and her hips thrust softly upward to meet the short, tight movements of his cock massaging her, teasing her to the edge of control.

"Come with me, Jess. Come now."

He felt the moment her breath held, her arms rigid and still, locked around him like iron . . . and then, and then, and then the sudden intense rush of release. Her fingers raked down his back as she screamed his name, pulsing in wild, arrhythmic waves around him.

Something inside Alex, something that kept his emotions protected and carefully in check during sex, *shattered*. His heart burst open with love for her. Fireworks exploded behind his eyes as he growled a guttural version of her name, pumping in violent, convulsive spurts before falling, limp and sated, across her beloved body.

Jessie's eyes opened sometime later to find Alex still slumped against her, his breathing more even than before, exhaling in hot puffs against her damp neck.

Having sex with Alex wasn't remotely like anything else she'd ever experienced before. His body was a tool, a masterpiece of pleasure, knowing exactly what to do to pull the maximum pleasure from hers. She had wondered how they would fit together, and Jess had her answer now. They were made for each other, like missing pieces of a puzzle that should never, ever be separated again.

Her eyes burned as she heard his words in her head: *You love me, don't you?* When she answered that she did, she had been out of her head, immersed in sensation, unable to weigh the timing of her assent. But even now, as she anticipated regret, she didn't feel it. Did she love Alex? Of course. Yes was the only answer she could have given.

Her arms were still loosely draped around his neck, and her fingers moved lazily through the soft tendrils of his hair. He reached down and pulled off the condom, leaning over her to throw it away. His arm remained heavy across her chest as he resettled himself beside her, his ear resting over her heart as she resumed running her fingers through his golden hair.

"That was . . . epic," he finally murmured, his lips moving softly over the skin of her chest, his arm still holding her tight. "The best. Ever."

She grinned, taking a deep breath and sighing. "Mm-hm."

And yes, coming from Alex English, she couldn't help but feel a little chuffed. Her worries from before—about competing with the other women who had shared his bed—were silenced now. Whoever they had been to him, she was here now, and he couldn't have faked the sort of pleasure she'd just given him.

"Can I ask you something?"

"Of course," she said.

"Are you okay with everything that just happened between us?"

"Mm-hm. You surprised me," she whispered. "A lot. You were so loving, Alex. So careful with me. You made me feel . . . cherished."

"Then why were you so sad?"

She didn't want to come off as some clingy, desperate girl, but lying naked in his arms, she couldn't bear to lie to him either. "Because being with you feels so good, so right, it's going to hurt to say good-bye. I know we said Christmas, but . . ."

He leaned on his elbow to look at her, his hand trailing to her heart, where it rested, firm and soothing. "Me too."

"You too?" she asked, uncertain of his meaning.

"I can't imagine saying good-bye to you," he whispered, tightening his arm around her.

She took a deep breath, nodding with relief, and threw her arm over her eyes to hide her tears. What was the matter with her? She was generally a levelheaded, even-keeled person, but her emotions were all over the place with Alex. Euphoric, loving, devastated, yearning, unable to be satisfied, even though she knew he was making exceptions for her that he never made for anyone else. What they had shared should be enough for her, and yet she wanted more *from* him, more *of* him, more time, more—

"Hey, Jess," he said, interrupting her thoughts.

"What?"

"We don't have to do anything we don't want to do."

"What do you mean?"

"I mean . . . we're adults. We have resources. We don't have to say good-bye if we don't want to. We'll figure it out."

She lowered her arm, swiping it over her eyes to catch her tears before looking at him hovering over her. His hair was damp against his forehead, and his eyes—full of love for her—were so achingly beautiful. She longed to believe him.

"We will?"

"Yeah. Christmas is just a day. What I feel for you isn't going to shut off like a faucet on December 26."

Her eyes swam. "What you feel for me?"

"I'm crazy about you, Jess."

"You are?" Her grin started small, but she couldn't help the way it took over her face.

"I am," he replied softly, sliding his hand to her breast, cupping it, letting his thumb brush over her nipple, which puckered for him instantly. He chuckled softly, smiling first at it, then at her.

She gave him a saucy smile. "You know, Alex English, you promised to make me come half a dozen times tonight."

"Did I say that?" he asked, rolling the erect flesh between his fingers.

Her heart quickened, and her muscles flexed in anticipation. "Mm-hm. And by my count, two down means—"

"Four to go," he murmured, rolling back on top of her and claiming her lips with his.

Chapter 10

Alex made good on his promise, and they fell—exhausted and happy—into a deep sleep before waking up to reach for each other on Sunday morning too. After a quiet brunch of omelets at his apartment, they visited ICA, where they walked around hand in hand for hours. Jessie tried to teach Alex something about modern art despite the way he kissed her and touched her and whispered salacious things into her ear that made her flush with pleasure and lose her train of thought.

With Jessie's fears about the other women assuaged and her sadness about leaving him soothed by his promise that they would figure it out, she was finally able to relax again. And what he did to her body—*ohmygod, ohmygod*—she was barely able to think about it without blushing. After four more times on Saturday night and three more on Sunday, she was surprised she could walk by the time she arrived home to Westerly on Monday morning.

She wasn't there to stay, though—she was only there to pack a little bag and return to the city. Alex had asked if she would stay over a few more nights. Without giving it a second thought, Jessie had agreed, desperate not to lose a moment with him, already jealous of the hours he spent at the office without her.

They found their own routine as the days moved forward. Jessie spent the days decorating their Christmas tree, meeting old friends for lunch, and visiting her mother at Westerly when her brothers were at work. And when Alex came home at night, he'd swoop her into his arms and drag her to his bed, stripping out of his clothes and pulling off hers on the way. And though they didn't say "I love you" to each other, every touch, every word, every kiss and sigh and breath shared what they already knew: every day they fell more deeply.

On Thursday morning, Alex woke Jessie by kissing the bridge of her nose, followed by the corners of her eyes, the patch of skin under her ear, and then the flume over her lips. Every morning since Sunday he had woken her up by kissing obscure places on her body—the tip of her elbow, the soft skin of her forearm, the web between her thumb and forefinger, the mole on the back of her neck, the birthmark on her hip, her belly button, the tip of her pinkie—areas he said that only a fool would ignore, because every part of her was perfect. Obscure kisses had quickly become her favorite part of waking up in Alex's bed every morning. She never knew what part of her body would be honored that day, but it meant every day started with a reminder that he treasured her.

"Good morning, girlfriend," he said, grinning when she opened her eyes.

"More," she murmured.

"You already got your four," he said, laughing softly at her greediness.

She blinked at the alarm clock on the bedside table.

"It's six thirty. You're already dressed." She pouted.

"I have to prepare for an early morning meeting, but I didn't want to leave without saying good-bye."

She took a deep breath and sat up, accepting the cup of coffee he offered, prepared just as she liked it, with a little milk and a smidgen of sugar.

"I won't be here when you get home."

His whole face changed from lighthearted to concerned. "Are you going home?"

"It's girls' night," she said, then bit her lip. "But wait, do you . . . do you want me to go home?"

"No," he answered simply.

She relaxed, taking another sip of coffee.

"So, girls' night, huh? Is that basically just an excuse for you and Emily and Daisy to drink beer and talk about me and my brothers?"

"Pretty much," she answered, winking at him. "Emily's roommate is coming too. Umm, Veronica?"

"No. Valeria."

Suddenly Jessie's heart started pounding, and she felt her smile fall. "You know her?"

"Sure, she's Emily's roommate."

"Alex," she repeated, trying to ignore the rolling of her stomach. "Do you *know* her?"

He stared at her for a long moment, before his eyes widened in understanding, and he shook his head. "No. Not like that."

"Phew," said Jessie, her shoulders relaxing as she took another sip of coffee. When she looked at him, his lips were a thin line and his brows were furrowed.

"Are you still worried? About the women I knew before you?"

She shook her head, hating the hurt on his face, determined not to make a big deal about something like this again. It did still bother her when she thought of Alex with someone else. But he couldn't change his past, and she couldn't get paranoid every time they went out. Part of her just wished that they never had to leave the safe, loving haven of his apartment.

"No. I promise I'm not. When you corrected me . . . about her name, I just . . . I just thought that maybe . . ."

He gave her a tight smile. "I understand."

"And you're playing squash today," she said a little too brightly, hoping to change the subject for the better and failing wildly.

"Aw!" he exclaimed. "I forgot all about that."

Jessie cringed. Just five minutes ago he'd woken her up looking flirty and happy, and now he was like a thundercloud. *Way to go, crappy girlfriend.*

"It won't be that bad."

"No? Because last I checked, you're practically living here, and they're not real happy about it. Have they stopped calling?"

They hadn't. Her brothers texted and called several times a day to share their disappointment and disapproval with her for shacking up with Alex English. She was doing a good job ignoring them on the surface, but it bothered—and hurt—her that they couldn't respect her choices as an adult woman.

She shook her head.

Alex crossed his room, rummaging through the top drawer of his bureau.

"What are you doing?"

"Looking for my jockstrap, Jess. My parts are extra valuable to me lately."

"Me too. They're my *favorite* parts. Ever."

He turned around and faced her with his hands on his hips, so handsome in a navy suit and crisp, white shirt that her heart skipped a beat. His tongue darted out to wet his lips as a smile spread across his face.

Just watching him, Jessie's heart took flight, and her own smile answered his.

"Do all couples have these sort of problems out of the gate?" he asked tenderly, holding her eyes as he walked back to the bed and sat down beside her.

She placed her coffee on the nightstand and scooted next to him, curling up against his chest. The sheet slipped away to bare her breasts, and she looked down at where her nipples grazed the front of his shirt every time she took a breath. When she looked back up at Alex, his eyes were dark and hungry.

"Fast," gasped Jessie, whipping the rest of the sheet away.

Alex's hand flew to the front of his dress pants, which he unzipped, pulling out his hard, huge erection. Grabbing a condom from the pile beside her coffee, he rolled one on quickly, then reached for Jessie, pulling her to the very edge of the bed and drawing her legs straight up against his crisp, white dress shirt until her ass felt the fabric of his pants against her skin.

"You want?" he panted, reaching down to line up his sex with hers.

"I *need.*"

Without waiting another moment, he grasped her thighs and thrust into her.

"Alex!" she cried, as the tip of his sex touched her womb.

"Jesus, Jess, you're always so wet for me." He sighed, drawing back before plunging into her again.

"That's because I always . . . want you. I'd live with you . . . inside me, if I could," she managed between pants.

"Fuck, Jess, you're going to make me come."

"That's the point," she gasped, gripping the edge of the mattress with her fingers. "But not yet."

"So hot," he groaned.

"So good," she answered.

An instinctive rhythm took over as Jessie closed her eyes, concentrating on the feeling of him sinking in, then pulling back, then sinking into her again. She tightened her internal muscles around him and felt him gasp aloud, swelling even bigger within her. Every time he thrust, her ass rubbed up against the dress material of his suit pants again, and she thought she might lose her mind—it was so sexy knowing that he'd wear those pants all day after her ass had been slamming against them this morning as he drove into her over and over again.

Alex reached forward to cup her breasts, squeezing the already erect nipples until the building pressure just below her belly exploded, and she bucked forward, sucking Alex as deep as she could while spasms of pleasure pulsed through her. Through the haze of her own orgasm, she heard him tense up and groan her name, finally slowing his rhythm within her, parting her legs and falling forward between them onto her chest. Half on the bed and half off, his chest was heavy on hers, and his head rested against her neck as he tried to catch his breath.

He pressed his lips to the skin of her throat, and then, out of nowhere, he said it.

"I love you, Jess."

She gasped, her hands on his back stilling in surprise.

"Jess?"

"I . . . I love you too," she whispered, as her eyes filled with tears.

His lips pressed against her neck again, and he rested his forehead against her skin as he always did before leaving her. It was Alex's way of wishing he didn't have to say good-bye.

Finally he braced himself on the mattress and stood, disposing of the condom and zipping up his pants before turning back to her with an adorable smile.

Jess had scooted back against the pillows, lying on her side, naked and on display.

"How am I supposed to leave you when you're looking at me like that?" he asked, frowning.

"One foot in front of the other," she suggested.

"Where are you going for girls' night?"

"Mulligan's."

"Lots of college guys hang out there," he grumbled.

"Lucky us," Jessie teased. "Maybe that's why Emily chose it."

"What if I showed up?"

She chuckled, rolling her eyes at him. "Don't trust me?"

"I trust you implicitly. I don't trust them."

She crawled over to where he stood, hands on his hips at the edge of the bed. Kneeling up, she rubbed her breasts against his white shirt and bit his bottom lip, then sat back on her haunches.

"I'm fairly certain Barrett and Fitz were going to invite you. Emily said they always show up uninvited. It's almost *part* of girls' night now."

"Will you still want me if Cameron breaks my balls off playing squash?"

"I'll still want you no matter what," she answered honestly, then shrugged. "But I'll have one less brother if he actually hurts you."

He leaned down and kissed her lips hard, telling her what she meant to him, that she belonged to him, that he owned her heart as surely as she owned his, and that there was only room for her in his life. She felt it. She knew it was true.

He turned to leave, but as he reached the doorway, he pivoted and caught her eyes with his.

"What I said before? I meant it, Jess."

"Me too," she said, wondering how it was that every time she thought her heart was full, Alex managed to find a little more space to call his own.

"Do you think I have a death wish? Hell, no, I'm not playing squash with you and the Winslows. What do you think I am, crazy?"

Alex grimaced at Stratton over his desk. "Please, Strat? They want to play doubles."

"They want to play Kill Alex. Just cancel."

"I can't cancel, and let me tell you something, little brother. If you don't come with me and convince Chris to go to Devon for the Harrison–Lowry merger, you're going to have to go."

"To England?" asked Stratton, reaching up to straighten his glasses in a nervous gesture Alex knew well. Stratton wasn't a big fan of international travel—he preferred the familiarity of home.

Alex nodded. "Barrett's getting married. Fitz is having a baby. Cam and I are the money. If Chris won't go, it's all you."

"What about Wes?"

"He hasn't even passed the bar yet. He's wet behind the ears, Strat. At least you've managed big mergers before."

"Not well," he said honestly. "I'm not the strongest option."

"You might be the *only* option if Chris won't go."

An hour later, Alex and Stratton pulled up in front of the Racquet Club of Philadelphia, with Stratton grumbling loudly about how much easier it would have been to have been born an only child.

They suited up, both of them donning new jockstraps that Alex had rushed out to buy while grabbing lunch. He didn't know what use Strat had for his balls, but Alex and Jessie had only three weeks left together, and he sure as hell wasn't going to let a squash game take him out of commission. He had a brief, intense flashback to taking her on the edge of the bed while fully dressed this morning, then grimaced as his cock twitched. Damn it, but she was the hottest, sweetest, sexiest girl he'd ever known. And by some miracle of fate, she loved his sorry ass. She said so. His heart swelled as he heard the words in his head from this morning.

He had to figure out a way to get her to stay. Perhaps
Barrett knew someone at ICA who could pull strings to get
Jessie a job there. He couldn't let her go. He couldn't bear
the idea of losing her.

"You ready to die?" asked Stratton, nudging Alex in the
hip, a sour look on his face.

Alex rolled his eyes and nodded, following his brother
out of the locker room.

Entering court three, they found Chris and Cam already
there, taking practice shots. As the door opened, Chris
turned to say hello, but Cam smashed a straight drive into
the front wall, which whizzed back toward Alex and Stratton, missing Strat's head by an inch.

"Oh, hell, no!" he said, turning around and walking back
out the door, leaving Alex alone with the Winslows.

Cam watched from the front of the court. "That wasn't
meant for Stratton."

Alex shrugged. "Are we playing? Should I go after him?"

"She's practically *living* with you," said Cam, his face taut
and furious.

"Calm down, Cam," warned Christopher, the peacemaker,
who didn't actually look very peaceful.

Alex glanced out the clear glass to the viewing area and
saw Stratton watching the conversation. For as much as Strat
probably wished he could leave, Alex knew he wouldn't,
and if either of the Winslows laid a hand on Alex, Stratton
would be back on the court with a vengeance.

Cam approached Alex, stopping in the center of the court
and pointing his racket at him. "You know what I don't get?
You could have any girl in Philly. Any girl. Why does it have
to be my sister?"

Alex glanced back at Stratton, who stood at attention, his
legs spread and planted, ready to sprint to Alex's defense. He
loved his brother for it. He understood how Cam felt. If anyone

tried to mess with Barrett, Fitz, Stratton, or Weston, they wouldn't live to tell about it if Alex could help it. He understood that Cam was only trying to protect Jessica because he loved her. The thing is? Alex loved her too. It was the only answer that mattered.

"I love her," said Alex, holding Cameron's grass-green eyes. "It has to be her because I'm in love with her."

Cameron stared at him, his face redder and redder as he huffed and postured. "Screw you, Alex."

"It's the truth."

"You love her. What a crock of shit. I should beat your head in with this racket. I should—"

The door opened, and Stratton slipped back into the room, standing against the back wall of the court with his arms crossed over his chest.

"Shut up, Cam," said Chris quietly, turning to Alex, his eyes narrow but searching. "Really? You love Jessica?"

Alex looked at Chris, realizing, for the first time, how similar he looked to Jess. They had the same lips, the same eye shape, the same long, black lashes.

"Yeah. I do."

"You sound serious."

"I am."

"Don't listen to him, Chris. He's practically a gigolo. He's—"

"She lives in London," stated Chris, ignoring his older brother. "If you love her, what's your plan?"

Alex clenched his jaw because as much as he wished he had an answer for Chris, he didn't. "We don't know yet."

"Just living from day to day, eh, Alex?" sneered Cam. "Who gives a crap if you break my sister's heart as long as you get what you want in the short term?"

"Screw *you*, Cameron. I didn't just meet her last week. Jess and I have history. This started a long time ago."

"Did you touch her when she was a little girl?" growled Cameron, his face murderous.

"No! God, you're such a douche bag! I was there for her—when your father died."

Cameron's face flushed purple as he rushed at Alex, but Stratton and Chris stepped in the way. Chris held his brother around the waist as Cam yelled, "You don't talk about my father while you're fucking my sister!"

Alex lurched toward Cam, reacting to his vulgar comment about Jess, ready to punch his lights out, but Stratton grabbed his arm firmly. "Time to go, Al."

"Get off me, Strat."

"Can't do it. Let it go, or I'll drag you out."

Cam continued to struggle against Chris as Alex wrenched himself away from Stratton. He picked up his racket and exited out a side door, cursing the entire situation. If Alex and the Winslows couldn't even play a round of squash together, how the hell were they supposed to work on the Harrison–Lowry merger? How were he and Jessica supposed to build a future together? He chewed on these troubling questions as he stood in the elevator, groaning as he got off at English & Sons.

As if his day could get any worse, Hope Atwell was waiting for him in the lobby.

"Hope?"

"Asshole," she greeted him acidly, with a sweet smile.

His eyes widened as he suddenly remembered their standing Thursday date. He'd cleared his calendar except for Hope. Damn it. He put his hand in the small of her back, guiding her to his office before she could make a scene.

After his office door closed, she turned to him. "I waited over an hour."

"I'm sorry."

"What the hell, Alex? We've been meeting for a year! You've never missed a Thursday unless it was a holiday."

Alex moved quickly to the wet bar, pouring her a glass of water and handing it to her. They sat down on his couch facing each other.

"I'm sorry."

"Stop saying you're sorry. What's going on with you?"

"I've met someone."

"You *what*?" she gasped, setting the water down on the coffee table in front of her.

"I've met someone."

Hope stared at him for several seconds before bursting out laughing. "So what?"

"So she's . . . special."

"I'm sorry," said Hope, cocking her head to the side. "But what the hell does she have to do with us?"

"I'm with her now. Only her. I don't, um, I don't want to see you anymore."

Hope's mouth dropped open.

"Are you *kidding* me?"

Alex shook his head, feeling genuinely bad for Hope. "No. I'm not. I'm in love with her."

Hope started laughing again, her shoulders shaking as she shook her head back and forth. "In *love* with her? Oh, Alex, that's precious. Does she know who you are? Practically a dick for hire!"

Alex refused to let Hope get under his skin. He took a deep breath, standing up and walking over to his desk. "She knows."

"What woman with any self-respect would put up with that?"

He turned to face her, resting his knuckles on his desk behind him. "I don't know, Hope. I'd ask you what sort of self-respecting woman would fuck me on a weekly basis with no commitment and no hope for the future, but that might hit too close to home."

Hope sprang up from the couch and approached Alex, her pretty face scrunched up and bright red. "You're a bastard!"

"So I've heard."

"I wasted a year on you."

"I don't remember you complaining."

"You English boys . . . you're *disgusting*."

Alex stared at her, refusing to engage anymore.

She wet her lips, cocking her head to the side again, and giving him a flirtatious smile. "So . . . you won't miss *this*?"

In a flash, she had her arms wrapped around his neck and her lips pressed against his. He kept his mouth tightly closed, but before he could reach up and pull her arms from his neck, he heard his door open.

"Oh, Alex, I didn't realize . . ."

Alex looked up to see Barrett's fiancée, Emily, standing in the doorway.

"Emily!" he gasped, taking Hope's wrists and pushing her away from him.

"I see you're busy."

"No," he insisted. "No, I'm not."

Hope turned, swiping the back of her hand across her lips. "Emily. You're Emily Edwards."

Emily nodded. Hope snorted. "My sister Felicity sends her regards."

Emily stepped into the room, her blue eyes steely and firm as she stared back at Hope. "I don't have a problem with Felicity."

"Your fiancé, Barrett, screws her and dumps her, but *you* don't have a problem. How nice for you."

Hope turned back to Alex. "If you change your mind . . ."

"I won't," said Alex. "Don't come here again."

"Asshole," muttered Hope, sneering at Emily as she brushed past her, out of Alex's office, and hopefully out of his life.

Emily took a deep breath, closing Alex's office door. "Detangling is never easy."

"She was my last loose end," said Alex.

Emily grinned at him, plucking a tissue from the box on his coffee table and offering it to him. "Your loose end wears very red lipstick."

Alex took the tissue gratefully, walking to the mirror over the wet bar.

"Thanks for interrupting," he said over his shoulder.

"No problem. But I need a favor."

"Anything."

"My roommate, Valeria. She's in a little bit of a jam."

"How so?" he asked. Aside from a small red smudge on his collar, he was well rid of Hope's lipstick. He turned back to Emily.

"The bank is threatening to shut down *Danse Allegre*, her aunt's dance studio. Val moonlights there for extra money, and, well, we love *Zia* Angelina, but we don't think she's managed her money very well. Barrett said you might be willing to look at her books for me? See if there's anything you can suggest?"

Alex nodded. "Absolutely. Can you get copies of everything? I'll have Stratton take a look first if that's okay. He combs through numbers faster than I do, and he even catches things I miss sometimes. Anyway, he and I will pow-wow after we each take a look, okay?"

Emily reached for Alex's hand and squeezed it. "I love this family, you know."

Alex winked, squeezing her hand back before dropping it gently. "For the record, this family loves you too, Emily Almost-English."

She waved good-bye, promising to forward the files soon, but as soon as she was gone, Alex's mood spiraled back to the dark place it had been before. He and Cam couldn't be in the same room together without throwing punches, he never got a chance to ask Chris about Devon, and Hope Atwell was sure to stir up trouble. Not to mention, Jess was supposed to leave for London three weeks from tomorrow, the very thought of which was enough to rip his beating heart out of his chest.

He shook his head back and forth, sitting down at his desk. The brightest spot in his sorry life was Jessica. His face softened as he heard her words in his head, *I love you too.* He needed to figure out how to get her to stay, because letting her go was unthinkable.

Chapter 11

The cab ride from Alex's apartment building to Mulligan's took only a few minutes, but it was enough time for Jessie to read the messages her brothers had sent that afternoon. Cam and Chris had both texted their almost fight with Alex on the squash court, calling him a maniac, and Brooks had left a long voice mail about family obligation and general disappointment. But the silver lining was a message from her mother that encouraged her to stay strong. Jessie grinned at that one. Her brothers were pouting and posturing, but they all liked Alex deep down inside. Once they understood that he loved her and he wouldn't hurt her, they'd back off. She was sure of it.

She scrolled through her voice messages, deleting most of them, but surprised that she'd missed one from this afternoon. It was from an unknown number, but the caller had left a message. She pressed *Listen*, holding her phone to her ear.

"Jessica? It's Hope Atwell. You don't know me, but my sister is Connie Atwell, who's friends with Jane Story, who learned from her sister Margaret that you're Alex English's new fuck buddy." Jessica gasped, lowered the phone, pausing the message. Alex had warned her that something like this would eventually happen, but she didn't feel prepared for someone to speak with such hostility and disrespect about her private life. It was so jarring, she rolled down the cab's window, taking a deep breath before pressing *Play* again. "When Alex and I got together today, things got a little hot between us. You see, Thursday's my day with Alex. We have a standing date at the Four Seasons. I just thought you should know. You take care, Jessica. Bye, now."

Jessica pressed *End* on her phone, letting it fall from her fingers into her purse. She tried to swallow the lump in her throat, but her eyes watering only made it bigger. *Things got a little hot . . . Thursday's my day . . . a standing date at the Four Seasons . . .*

"No," she murmured, fisting her hands in her lap. She and Alex were exclusive. He loved her. He'd said so.

Her face softened as she recalled his last words as he left her this morning. *What I said before? I meant it, Jess.* She took a deep breath, forcing her racing heart to calm down. Alex had warned her that jealous exes could reach out to her when they found out that Alex had a girlfriend. That's all this was. Jessie was quite sure that it was all a lie—Hope probably hadn't seen Alex at all. She was lying.

This is just a disappointed, angry woman lashing out because she can't have the man she wants. My *man.*

She thought about calling Alex to find out if any of it was true, but remembered his face this morning when she asked him about Valeria. He didn't need her distrust right now. They needed to be strong together against people like Hope Atwell, who wanted to pull them apart.

The cab pulled up at Mulligan's, and Jessie paid the driver. Though she was determined not to let Hope ruin her girls' night out, she'd be lying if she said she was unaffected by the phone message. It had taken a little shine off the evening. That was the truth.

Still, she fixed a smile on her face and walked into the college bar, finding Emily, Daisy, and their friend Valeria sitting together at a table in the back.

Emily waved her over, and Jessie wound her way through the crowd, sliding into the booth beside Daisy.

"Hey, Jessie!" exclaimed Emily, grinning at her from across the table. "You look great!"

Jessie looked down at her ensemble: a simple white button-down shirt tucked into belted skinny jeans with knee-high brown leather boots. She shrugged out of her navy blue cropped jacket, laying it over her bag, and grinned, her worries about Hope and Alex dissipating as she surrounded herself with girlfriends.

"Yeah? Thanks. I copy everything Kate Middleton wears," she said, sharing her secret.

"I copy all her shoes," said Valeria from beside Emily. "I don't think I could get these hips into any of her clothes. By the way, I'm Val."

Jessie shook her hand across the table. "Jess. And two things, Val. One, she has some *awesome* shoes. And two, I'd *kill* for your curves."

"From what I hear, Alex likes *your* curves just fine."

Emily and Daisy giggled as Jessie's eyes flew open and her cheeks flushed.

"I guess he does," she confessed.

"Don't mind Val," said Daisy, nudging Jessie in the side. "She just says what we all think."

"Can I be really vulgar and nosy?" asked Val.

Jessie shrugged. She knew she was among friends. "Sure."

"Is he as good as they say?"

Jessie's mouth dropped open in surprise, but she couldn't help smiling and nodding. "Way better."

"Gah!" exclaimed Val, palming her forehead with one hand and lifting her pint glass with the other. "I have to get me an English boy!"

"Stratton and Weston are still free," said Jessie, grinning at Emily to thank her for the glass of beer she slid across the worn wooden table.

"Weston's a baby," said Val dismissively, "but Stratton English . . . oh my God. He showed up here a few weeks ago, and I almost died. He's so hot."

"Remember *that* night, Daze?" asked Emily, grinning at her cousin like the Cheshire cat.

"Perfectly," said Daisy, blushing as she sipped her soda.

"What happened?" asked Jessie, sensing a story.

"I admitted that I wasn't engaged, and Fitz dragged me into the back hallway," Daisy said, flicking her chin toward the back of the bar before turning to Jess askance. "Best. Kiss. Ever."

"The electricity on this half of Philly got a boost from the current," said Val, matter-of-factly, chugging the rest of her beer and sliding it to Emily who poured her a fresh one.

Daisy giggled again, spreading her hands over her belly.

"Are you feeling better?" asked Jess.

"I am. Eight weeks, and everything's settling down now. Sweet Pea's the size of a raspberry," she added, smiling.

"Sweet Pea? That's so cute!"

Daisy smiled. "You know that song? *Sweet pea, apple of my eye . . .*"

"*. . . you're the only reason I keep on coming home*," sang Jess quietly. "I love that song."

"Me too," said Daisy, her smile far away, as if remembering something really nice. "We're dancing to it at the wedding. This one's helping us learn some moves."

Valeria smiled back at Daisy, then turned to Jessie. "My aunt owns a dance studio. I do some moonlighting there."

"How fun! I'm a terrible dancer."

"I bet Alex doesn't think so."

Jessie grinned, thinking back to the night on the balcony at the Union League Club, when they danced to "The Way You Look Tonight."

"I knew it!" said Val triumphantly.

Jessie giggled, shaking her head at Val and turning to Emily. "How are the wedding plans coming along?"

"Well, we were planning to have a double wedding in June, but this one got herself knocked up, so . . ."

"So Fitz and I are going to get married on Valentine's Day," said Daisy.

"And Barrett and I will wait for June, as planned."

"Valentine's Day! That's so soon!"

Daisy smiled. "Will you come back for it, Jessie?"

"Sure," she answered softly.

Jessie knew she dropped her eyes too quickly, but the question made her heart clench with uncertainty. Would she and Alex still be together two months from now? Her heart insisted that they would be, but her mind wasn't convinced. They'd barely discussed their plans for after Christmas.

"Hey, Jess. You okay?" asked Emily.

"Yeah," she said, forcing a smile.

"How are you and Alex doing?"

"He told me that he loved me this morning," she said softly.

"You love him too?" asked Daisy.

Jessie nodded. "Always have."

"Another English brother bites the dust," mourned Val.

"So . . . that's good, right? He loves you, you love him, the sex is amazing . . ."

"It's good, yeah." Jessie looked at Emily, wincing as she shook her head. "I'm ridiculous. I have this gorgeous, amazing guy telling me he loves me, and all I can think about is that I have to go back to London in three weeks."

"Do you *have* to go back?" asked Emily. "You have dual citizenship, right?"

"Right. But, I live there. It's my *home*. I haven't lived in Philly since I was a little girl, you know? You guys are so great, and Westerly is so beautiful . . . but I don't feel like I belong here. Not like I do there."

Emily nodded and said softly, "And Alex belongs here."

"He's the CFO of English & Sons. And he *loves* it here. His family's here, and he adores Philadelphia, the Eagles, Haverford Park. I can't imagine him leaving."

Val huffed lightly. "Sorry to be Captain Obvious, but one of you is going to have to give if you want it to work. I mean, long distance from New York to Philly would be one thing, but from London to Philly?"

"I know. We just haven't figured it out yet." Jessie sighed, hating the heaviness that threatened to overtake her good mood. "Hey, I'm getting sad. Can we talk about something else?"

"Definitely," said Daisy. "I had a dream last night that I was attacked by a fifty-foot squid. My dreams have gotten really weird."

"*Normale*," said Valeria in her native Italian. "My sister's dreams were off the charts all nine months. It was like experiencing an acid trip every time she told us about them."

As Daisy and Valeria bantered back and forth about pregnancy and dreams, Jessie looked across the table at Emily, who gave her a sympathetic smile that didn't make Jessie feel better at all. Valeria was right. As much as she hated the thought, the only way she and Alex were going to work out was if one of them gave up their life for the other.

It put her new relationship under harsh light to look at it in such black-and-white terms. For all that their feelings had quickly moved from a childhood crush to love, it was still a newborn love that needed to be protected and nurtured. The stress of moving, the meshing of lives prematurely, could put too much pressure on it, threaten it, weaken it, destroy it. And yet wouldn't it be worse to be separated? To meet for a weekend every four weeks? To drift away from each other day by day as their lives swallowed them up again?

Jessie took a long gulp of her beer, biting her lip in thought until she was distracted by Emily saying Alex's name.

". . . so Alex said that Stratton would look at the numbers first, and then he'd take a look too. Hopefully they can help."

Valeria looked grateful, and Jessie asked, "Is Alex helping you with something?"

"My aunt doesn't manage her money very well, and the bank's threatening to call in the loan on her dance studio. I'm hoping the English brothers can figure out a miracle to save it."

"Stratton's the Great Fixer," said Daisy, using air quotes. "When Fitz and I first reconnected, I told him I wanted to start a bakery and voilà! Stratton had the entire thing pretty much figured out twelve hours later."

"Oooh! I have a problem with my vagina that needs fixing," deadpanned Valeria. "You think he could help me with that?"

Jessie, Emily, and Daisy whooped with laughter, none of them noticing that Barrett, Fitz, and Alex had all arrived a few minutes before and were standing up against the bar watching them.

"Me, you, or Barrett?" Alex asked Fitz, raising an eyebrow. "Which one of us are they laughing about?"

"Could be Stratton or Wes," said Barrett. "Or someone else entirely."

"Yeah, right. None of them is in the bedroom with Stratton or Wes. Stop being an idiot, Barrett." He leaned his elbow on the bar and narrowed his eyes. "Seriously. What do you think they're saying?"

"I have no clue," said Fitz, his face going all soft. "Look at my girl drinking Sprite. Damn, I love that woman."

"It's nice that she doesn't want your kid to come out with thirteen toes."

"Yeah," said Fitz, grinning at Alex. "She's sweet like that."

"Don't you guys think Emily's superhot?" asked Barrett, staring at his fiancée as he tipped back his bottle and took a long pull.

"Awkward," said Alex.

"All Edwards girls are gorgeous," said Fitz diplomatically, clinking Barrett's bottle with his. "You know, Bar, our kids are going to be almost like genetic siblings. Wild, right?"

Barrett shook his head. "I'm not thinking about kids yet. I don't want anyone walking in on me and my hot wife. I want her all to myself for a while."

"Amen, brother," said Alex under his breath, saluting his oldest brother with his bottle, then taking another gulp of cold beer.

"How are things with Jessie?" asked Fitz.

"Good."

"But not so good with the Winslows," observed Barrett. "Cam called today threatening to bow out of the deal. It took me an hour to calm him down. For now, they're still in, and I think I convinced Christopher to be project manager. But no thanks to you."

"Sorry, Barrett. Things got a little haywire at squash today."

Barrett's eyes flicked to Alex's collar. "And Emily said that she walked in on you kissing Hope Atwell."

"No! No no no! Crap! Is that what she th—"

"Chill out. She said it wasn't your fault, that you were pushing Hope away."

"I don't know why I ever got involved with her. Ugh. The Atwells."

"Amen, brother," said Barrett, drinking to Alex.

"She had some choice words for Emily."

"I heard," said Barrett, his lips thin and annoyed. "But my woman's tough. She can take it. Hope Atwell's no match for Emily Edwards."

"I'm well rid of her."

"Can you just get your shit in order, please? Jessie . . . the Winslows . . . all of it. Time to grow up, Alex."

"I'm working on it."

"Hey, what do you guys think of Valeria Campanile?" asked Fitz, checking out Emily's roommate.

Alex gave Fitz a look. "You're having a baby, man. I don't think you should be—"

"Don't be a moron, Al. For Strat."

"For *Strat*?" blurted out Alex. "Is he finally interested in someone?"

"I don't know," said Fitz, thoughtfully, taking another sip of beer.

Barrett shook his head. "Don't go messing around in Stratton's love life, Fitz. Leave him alone."

"Daisy thinks he's lonely."

"Maybe," said Alex, "but until Strat asks for help, I'm with Barrett. I think you should leave it alone."

"Hmm."

"Uh, excuse me?"

Alex, Fitz, and Barrett turned from watching their women to look at the bartender, who pushed three cold, open beers toward them. "Ladies at the end of the bar wanted you gentlemen to have another round."

Alex looked around Barrett to where three gorgeous women stood, beaming their prettiest, sexiest smiles at the English brothers. He recognized the one in the middle—*um, Alyssa? Yeah. Alyssa what?* He couldn't remember. She was a real yeller, though. He remembered that. She was someone he'd hooked up with a few months ago, and his stomach rolled over as he looked back over at Jessie, who was leaning across the table, saying something to Emily and Val that was making them all smile.

"Send them back," said Alex.

"What the hell, Al?" said Barrett. "Jesus, it's just a friendly gesture."

"Send them back," Alex told the bartender, flexing his jaw and pushing the beers away.

"They're already open. You may as well drink them."

"I'm not going to say it again," growled Alex.

The bartender shook his head but took the beers off the bar, putting them on the back counter behind him.

Alex didn't turn back to his brother until the beers were well out of reaching distance, but when he did, Fitz was beaming at him. "Now tell me you're not in love with her."

"Shut up, Fitz," said Alex, heading to the bathroom.

"Yep," said Fitz, from behind him. "That's what I thought."

Emily was the first to notice the brothers approaching.

"Daisy! Time!"

Daisy flipped over her phone and swiped the screen. "9:06."

"Wow," said Emily, grinning up at a ridiculously handsome Barrett, who looked over the moon to see her. "A whole hour and six minutes to ourselves."

"You want us to go?"

Emily shook her head.

"You can have my seat," said Val to Barrett, hopping up and giving him a kiss on the cheek before looking back down at Emily. "Can you two go to his place tonight? I have studying to do. I need quiet, if you know what I mean."

Emily's eyes widened like saucers, and she blushed bright red. "Val!"

"I've said it before, and I'll say it again: the walls are thin. Barrett?"

"*Il tuo desiderio è un ordine, Valeria,*" said Barrett in creditable Italian.

Jessie grinned at Val's slack-jawed, stunned expression, wondering if she might faint on the spot. Instead, she muttered something about "getting her own English brother," threw her messenger bag over her shoulder, and pushed between Barrett and Fitz to leave.

"What does that mean?" demanded Emily, her bright, blue eyes sparkling up at Barrett.

"'Your wish is my command,'" said Barrett in a low, suggestive rumble as he slid into the booth beside his fiancée. "I missed you."

"Maybe you *were* being serious about Barrett being the hottest," a voice whispered in Jessie's ear, and her heart leaped and danced as Polo Black surrounded her.

She looked up to see Alex sliding in beside her. "No chance. But you have to admit, player, that was pretty damn smooth."

"Player? I'm taken." Alex dropped his eyes to her mouth. "But I'll show you smooth."

He kissed her soundly, making her toes curl in her boots, pulling away just before things got indecent. He put his arm around her, shaking his head with a look of pure adoration. "Damn, Jess."

"Jesus, Al, get a room," teased Fitz, looking over at Daisy, who was sandwiched in the corner between Jessie and the wall. "How're you feeling, beautiful? How's Sweet Pea?"

"We're fine," she said, smiling back at him. "And guess what? I got a late day order for four hundred cookies!"

"Amazing! And in your first week too! My girl's one *phenomenal* businesswoman."

Barrett picked up his beer. "To Daisy's Delights."

They all picked up their glasses to cheers, and feeling happier than she could ever remember, surrounded by friends and the love of her life, Jessie snuck a quick peek at Alex's smiling face to her left. That's when she noticed it: the small, but unmistakable, smudge of red lipstick on Alex's collar.

When Alex and I got together today, things got a little hot between us . . . I just thought you should know.

Jessie gasped softly, staring at the smudge, the small sound of shock and pain overridden by the clanking of glass and congratulations to Daisy. Her chest heaved as all the air was suddenly sucked out of the room, and her stomach rolled over. Wondering if she was going to be sick, she clenched her jaw together, staring down at the table miserably.

"Jess," said Emily suddenly, "come to the bathroom with me?"

"Hey," said Alex, dipping his head to hers, "are you okay, baby? What's—"

Jessie looked up at Emily gratefully, then flicked her glance to Alex. "Let me out."

"Sure. I just . . ."

"Now, please."

"Jess, did something—"

He stood, and Jessie heard the worry in his voice, but she couldn't look at him. Between Hope's call and the lipstick on his collar, she was about to burst into tears, and she couldn't bear embarrassing herself like that. She kept her head down, sliding out of the booth and keeping her back to the table.

"Alex, just give us a minute," said Emily, putting her arm around Jessie's shoulders and leading her to the bathroom.

Jessie didn't look up, didn't see where they were going. She trusted Emily to lead her through the crowd and kept her eyes down, desperately holding the tears at bay. Once inside the bathroom, Emily closed and locked the dead bolt in the door, as Jessie slumped against the wall, taking a deep, shaky breath as tears spilled from her eyes.

"It's not what you think," said Emily.

"What do you mean?"

"The lipstick. On his collar. It's not what you think."

"How did you—"

"I saw your face. I know exactly where your mind went because mine would've gone to the exact same place."

Holding on to whatever shred of hope Emily could offer, Jessie swiped at her eyes, looking up at her friend's face. "What do you mean that it's not what I think?"

"Okay, can you listen?"

Jessie took a deep, jagged breath and nodded.

"I needed to talk to Alex today about Valeria's aunt's dance studio. I've gotten so used to visiting Barrett at the office, I hardly ever knock anymore. When I barged into Alex's office, Hope Atwell was throwing herself at Alex, and he was pushing her away. She said, 'If you change your mind . . . ,' and Alex said, 'I won't. Don't come here again.' Hope was really angry and tried to insult me a little, and then she left in a huff. Alex called her his last loose end. He didn't kiss her, Jessie. She was trying to kiss him, and I suspect some of her lipstick got on his collar as he pushed her away."

Jessie took a shaky breath, her hands fisting at her sides as she imagined any woman touching Alex now that he belonged to her. "You swear it?"

"Oh, Jess. Of course. I'd never defend someone who was in the wrong, I'd tell you to run. But Alex is in love with you. It's completely obvious."

Reassured, Jessie slumped against Emily, who held out her arms. She felt relieved about the lipstick but took a shaky breath before telling Emily about the phone call. "Hope left me a t-terrible voice message t-today, and I didn't want to b-believe it, but when I saw . . . when I saw the . . ."

"Hey," said Emily, rubbing her friend's back. "Any girl in a new relationship would have wondered the same."

Jessie took a deep, ragged breath as her tears ended, and Emily ran a piece of paper towel under cold water and handed it to her.

"He's been with a lot of women," said Jessie as she pressed the cool paper to her eyes, wiping away her streaked mascara and fanning her face.

"He has," said Emily quietly, without mincing words. "Can you handle it?"

"I don't—yes. I can," said Jess with more confidence than she felt. Inside she felt young and confused and unaccustomed to so much high emotion. But one feeling overshadowed the rest, and she shared it with Emily. "I have to. I love him."

Emily smiled at her, taking the paper towel from Jessie's hands and tossing it in the trash. "Talk to him about it. I know he'll reassure you."

Jessie sighed, running a hand through her hair, wondering—for the first time—if Alex's reassurances would be enough. She believed Emily, and she felt certain that Alex hadn't cheated on her with Hope, but the whole episode was so upsetting, and there was no way Alex could ensure that it wouldn't happen again.

"Ready to go back?"

Jessie nodded, putting her hand on Emily's arm. "Emily, thank you. So much."

"You never know," said Emily, grinning at her. "We could be sisters someday."

Jessie laughed softly and followed her friend out of the bathroom only to have her arm grabbed immediately upon exiting.

"Are you okay?" Alex asked, holding her tightly like she might run away from him, his concerned eyes searching hers.

Jessie looked at Emily, who gave Jessie a thumbs-up and mouthed "Good luck" before returning to the table.

"Jess?"

Taking a deep breath, she looked up at Alex. His eyes were dark and worried in the dim light of the corridor.

"You have lipstick on your collar."

"What?" He let go of her arm, pulling his collar away from his neck and looking down awkwardly. His eyes flared as he looked back up at her. "Jess, I swear, it's not what it looks like. Baby, I—"

"Shhhh." She put her palm against Alex's cheek, smiling at him gently. "I know. I already know. Emily told me. She walked in on you pushing Hope Atwell away and telling her that you didn't want to see her anymore."

He wrapped his arms around her, pulling her against his chest. "It's true."

"She . . . she, um, she called me today. Hope. Left me a pretty ugly message about how you two get together on Thursdays."

"We don't anymore," he said gravely, searching her eyes and tightening his grip around her.

"I believe you. I believe that she's in your past."

"And you're my future," he whispered into her ear, dropping his forehead to hers. "God, Jess, I'm sorry."

"You didn't do anything wrong, Alex. I'll get better at this. I promise."

"I'm yours, remember? I can't change my past, but you're the *only* girl for me." He kissed her lips gently. "I hate it that you got upset, Jess. I hate that you can't completely trust me."

"I do. I do, Alex," she said, pulling back to look at him. "I handled the phone call okay. But the lipstick . . . I just—"

"I know. I know how it must have looked. And I'm sorry that she called you," he said, his breath warm on her face. "This has been the worst day. Ever."

"I heard about squash. Doesn't sound like it went so well."

"Understatement of the year."

"They're just being protective. They don't understand what's going on between us, but I promise they'll come around," she said, cocking her head to the side and smiling at him. She couldn't bear to see him looking so defeated and tired. "Hey, today's not done yet. What could we do to make it better?"

"I can think of a few things," he said, leaning forward to press his lips to the side of her neck. "Home. Bed. You. Forget the rest of today ever happened."

She wet her lips, muscles deep inside her body clenching in anticipation. "Deal."

He pressed a kiss to her forehead before taking her hand and pulling her out of the corridor, into the crowd.

"We're going to head home," said Alex, stopping at their table and pulling Jess close to his side.

Emily grinned, her eyes questioning. Jessie winked at her in thanks.

"Yeah, we're not far behind," said Fitz, whose shoulder was occupied by a sleepy-looking Daisy.

"Join us again next week?" asked Emily, and Jessie was about to answer, when a low, sexy voice over her shoulder stole her attention.

"Hey, hot stuff," it purred.

GODDAMN IT.

This had to be the worst—the *very* worst—day of Alex's life.

He turned his head to find Alyssa-from-the-bar standing behind him. First Hope, now Alyssa. He would be lucky if Jessie didn't smack his face off his neck and run from him like her hair was on fire.

"Alyssa, right?" he asked through an uninviting sigh.

"Oh! You remember me!" Alyssa reached out to trail a finger down his arm. "We met at the—"

"I'm so sorry," said Jessie, taking Alyssa's finger off Alex's arm and using both of her hands to shake Alyssa's hello. "We haven't met. I'm Jessica Winslow."

Alyssa gave Jess a thin, annoyed smile, pulling her hand away. "Good for you." Then, turning back to Alex, she continued, "Polo '14 fund-raiser in—"

"I'm sorry, again," said Jess, flashing a bright smile at Alyssa. "*Love* polo, but we can't chat right now. We were just on our way out."

Alex looked at Jess, and his heart just about exploded. He *belonged* to her, and she was staking her claim. It was so unexpected and so hot, he chuckled lightly through shallow breaths, pulling her closer. Her eyes were fiery and bright, but her expression was so intense, no sane woman would be wise to tangle with her.

Clearly Alyssa was *in*sane.

"I wasn't really talking to you." She turned back to Alex. "So, Al—"

"I know you weren't. You were hitting on my boyfriend right in front of me . . . my boyfriend who can't even remember where he met you."

"I was about to remind him."

"Don't." Jessie took a step closer to Alyssa and lowered her voice. "I know he's beyond gorgeous, and I'm sure he gave you orgasms that you have been reliving for months. Is that about right?"

"Uh . . . Well, I'm . . . I don't—"

Jessica held up her hand. "I know. Really, I do. I sympathize, even. But here's the thing . . . he's not available anymore. He's taken."

Jessie turned to Alex, her eyes heavy under their artificial brightness. "Isn't that right?"

"That's right," he whispered, seeing the conflict on her face, the discomfort despite her bravado. She was holding her own externally, but he sensed she wasn't quite as confident inside.

She turned back to Alyssa. "We're finished here. Have a nice evening."

Then she flashed her green eyes back at him. Dark, but committed. Shaken, but terribly in love. He saw it all, and his heart clenched with tenderness edged with fear.

The only thing he knew was that they needed some time alone so he could remind her of everything he offered her: his heart, his body, his very soul, if she asked for it.

Without giving Alyssa or their wide-eyed friends another look, Alex slid his hand down until his fingers found hers, and without taking his eyes off her for a second, walked them out the front door, to the safe haven of home.

Chapter 12

The next two weeks were full of conflict for Jess.

On one hand they were full of Christmastime and Alex, two of her favorite things. Philadelphia was decked out in white lights, green trees, and red bows. Jessie marveled at her first American Christmas in over ten years. The decorations, the music, the constant good cheer—she soaked it up like the child she'd been when she'd last experienced a Philadelphia-style Christmas.

She also basked in her love for Alex, because she was certain of it. He had quickly become her everything, and nothing was more important than loving him, pleasing him, learning about him, spending every night tangled together, his body thrusting into hers until she fell asleep, limp and exhausted, in the familiar heaven of his arms. Alex had become her reason for breathing, and the moments she spent with him—completely alone in the perfect sanctuary of his apartment—were among the most precious of her life.

But the other hand, on which sat every other aspect of her life, was increasingly heavy. The strain became more exhausting each day.

All but alienated from her family, her brothers had given up on the texts and calls, and Jess had stopped visiting Westerly, tired of their lectures, disappointment, and disapproval. Her mother met her for lunch in the city every few days, but even her mother wasn't championing her relationship with Alex very much anymore: it had caused too much dissension in her family for Olivia Winslow to support with any cheerfulness. Though she still defended Jessica's right to make her own decisions, the price of losing her brothers was too high for her mother to countenance.

Not to mention, it had been four weeks since Jess left London, and she was desperately yearning for home. Alex had asked her to think about staying a few more weeks in Philadelphia, and though she told him she would consider it, the idea of staying longer, let alone relocating her life to the United States, sum and total, upset her whenever she turned her mind to it.

Part of the problem was that Jessie would be giving up her life in London for Alex's life in Philadelphia, and the reality was that she didn't love Alex's life in Philadelphia. Not at all.

Though she had grown to care deeply for Emily and Daisy, and would always have a deep affection for the English family, other old friends looked at her differently when they found out she was Alex's new girl. Hope wasn't the only ex of his who had been in contact with her. She'd received several devastating e-mails cloaked as well-meaning advice that warned her about Alex's history in lurid detail, and the two times she'd attended social events with Alex the weekend after the incident with Hope—once to the symphony and once to a party at the Union League Club—Jessie could sense the women with whom Alex had been intimate. Their eyes raked over his body with a familiarity she dreaded, shooting daggers of hatred at Jess, or snickering at her role as Alex's latest conquest. After those two disastrous evenings, she'd declined further invitations, telling herself what she and Alex had was so perfect they didn't need to attend flashy events for fun. They made their own fun with each other in the quiet of his apartment.

But society events weren't the only places where Alex attracted attention. Once, during a picture-perfect day of Christmas shopping, while they were having lunch alone at a little bistro, a woman who'd been with Alex approached their table to hit on him. Another time, while walking through the Japanese Garden, a previous lover had given him her card, suggesting a time they could "get together" again. Every time, Jessie did her polite, but firm, job of pissing on Alex's leg, but the experiences weren't strengthening her. They were *exhausting* her. It made her feel shrewish and hostile, and she was losing her spirit and lightheartedness in the process. It didn't make her love Alex any less, but it made his world infinitely less appealing than the one she'd left.

She'd known from the very beginning, of course, that loving Alex meant accepting his past, but she was ashamed to learn that acceptance was far easier in theory than in application. Jessie—who was quite the social butterfly in London—now dreaded social engagements and even simple outings, cajoling Alex to stay home with her instead. And while she loved their evenings at home, eating Chinese and watching cheesy Christmas movies, she knew she was hiding like a coward. And even though Alex never protested, she sensed that they were both missing the vibrant social lives they were quickly leaving behind.

The answer to the question of "What comes next?" wasn't forthcoming, but cloudier every day, and Jessie, who was used to a happy, uncomplicated life in London, became increasingly weary of her life in Philadelphia.

A few days before Christmas, she lay with Alex in his bed, sprawled across his chest as he stroked the bare skin of her back. He'd just made love to her for the second time that night, and her body was tired, even though her mind felt frenzied, jumbled with too many questions and not enough answers.

"Tell me what you're thinking about," said Alex. "The last day or two, you've been so distracted, I'm starting to worry."

"I'm thinking about us," she answered. "We haven't figured it out yet, and my ticket's for the twenty-sixth."

His hand stilled. "I hoped you were thinking about staying. Barrett called his contact at ICA, and she said that—"

"I . . . I'm still thinking about it." She sighed. "But I miss London. So much."

"I know, baby, and I've been thinking about it too. Let's go for a visit. I'll take a few days off between Christmas and New Year's. You can use your ticket. We can spend a few days and still be home by the first of the year."

"Can you take that time away from work?" she asked, leaning her chin on his chest and catching his eyes.

"Sure. Christmas week's usually quiet. Listen, I know how much you love to travel. We can go back and visit as much as you want, Jess." He swallowed, and Jess could tell he was gathering his courage to say something important. "But when we come home, I want you to move in with me."

Her mouth dropped open as she stared at him, speechless.

He'd promised her, the first night they made love, that he'd come up with a plan for them, and he had. And on paper, it was a good plan: move in together, live in Philadelphia where they both had family, visit London frequently. They'd share the apartment that she'd grown to love so well, and it even included a volunteer position at ICA arranged by Barrett. Alex had figured it out for them, and thoughtfully too. He'd figured out a way for them to stay together.

So why didn't Jess jump for joy? Throw her arms around him? Yell yes in ten different languages? Why did she feel so dreadfully scared and sad?

"Jess?" he prompted.

She forced the same smile she used to give Brooks when he told her to apply herself at school or try harder on the tennis team. "Wow. That's a plan."

Alex leaned up on his elbows, shimmying back against the pillows behind him so he could sit up straight. Jess rolled onto her side, propping herself on her elbow to look up at him, and he searched her eyes, crossing his arms over his chest.

"Though not, apparently, a plan you like," he said softly, disappointment and unpleasant surprise making his voice tight. "I've never asked anyone to live with me. I thought you'd be happy."

"I . . . Alex, I . . ." She wet her lips, looking down at the crisp white sheets where they'd just made love. "I *do* want to live with you. I love you so much."

"But you don't want to live with me *here*."

"I miss home," she said softly. "I miss the Tate and my friends and my little flat. I miss the food, if you can believe it, and the pubs. I miss Paris or Stockholm for the weekend. I miss my life there . . . *terribly*. Philadelphia feels so complicated. My brothers are still so angry with us, and . . ." She sighed, looking down again, as her voice trailed off.

"And what?"

Her eyes cut to his. "You *know* what."

His nostrils flared as he took a deep breath. "You knew what you were getting into with me, Jess. You knew about my past."

"I know," she said, her voice breaking because she felt so miserable. She could feel the change between them—the tough questions they couldn't answer, the insurmountable issues that even love couldn't conquer on its own.

"You insisted you could handle it," he said quietly, hurt infusing his voice.

"I thought I could."

He clenched his jaw like it hurt to swallow. "But you can't."

A tear rolled out of the corner of her eye and plopped onto the mattress as she shook her head. "It's changing me."

He flinched, his face a study in worry and pain. "What do you mean?"

"Alex . . ." She smiled wistfully. "At home, I love parties and outings. I'd love introducing you to people and seeing their eyes widen with curiosity or admiration as they added your face to their blank slate. I'd love holding your hand and passing people on the street who you didn't know, who'd never touched you." Her smile faded as another tear chased the first. "Here, it's different. I hate going out with you. I hate going to parties because I can tell who's slept with you. I hate seeing their eyes sweep over what belongs to me like it once belonged to them. I . . . I hate the e-mails and the phone calls warning me that you'll break my heart. I hate it that my brothers can't give you a chance because they still see the person you were, not who you are with me." She shook her head, letting the tears fall, adding herself to the list of everything she hated. "I feel like we need a fresh start, and I don't see how we can get it here."

"But we can get it in London," he said, his voice hard and angry.

"Have you slept with half of London?" she asked in a whisper.

He flinched, clenched his jaw, his eyes hard. "No. I haven't."

"I'm sorry I said that." She reached for his hand, but he didn't clasp hers when she took it. "Alex, I'm . . . I'm not saying this well."

"You're doing fine," he said. "But I have responsibilities here. I admire your volunteer work at the Tate, but I'm the CFO of one of the top investment firms on the East Coast, Jess. I can't just walk away from that."

"I know." Her pulse raced and her face flushed as the full weight of their conversation settled on her shoulders. "What are we . . . Alex, what are we doing here?"

"Talking."

"No," she said, shaking her head and sitting up. She pulled the comforter around her, covering her breasts. "What are we doing . . . right now?"

He stared at her for a long time, his jaw hard, his lips thin. Only the glistening brightness of his blue eyes betrayed the shattering of his heart.

"I think we're breaking up," he said in a tortured whisper before drawing a ragged breath and blinking his eyes.

"No, we're not," she insisted, wiping away her tears and crawling toward him. She cradled his face with her hands, looking into his brimming eyes. "We love each other."

Alex placed his hand over his heart, rubbing with the flat of his palm, like his chest was aching. "Maybe love isn't enough."

Jessie had just had the same exact thought a few minutes before, but hearing him say it was so painful, it ripped through her like no agony she'd ever known before. She'd been holding her breath, but now she exhaled in a sob, her shoulders shuddering as she stared into his face.

"Forget it. Forget everything I s-said," she begged him. "I'll move here. I'll f-figure out how to . . . be happy, to be, um, be stronger. I can try harder to ignore it. P-please, Alex. Please."

He reached for her hands, lowered them to his lap, his face stricken and devastated as he shook his head back and forth. "No, Jess. No, baby." He reached up to swipe at a tear that had slipped from his eye. "I can't let you do that. I can't let you be so unhappy for me. I can't let you change into someone else. I love you too much to let that happen."

Her mind raced frantically. He was the love of her life, and she wasn't going to lose him. There had to be a way.

"Then we'll, um, we'll f-fly back and forth. One weekend here, one in London. We c-could do that, couldn't w-we?"

His thumbs brushed gently against her wrists. "No, Jess. We couldn't do that. Not forever."

Her head fell forward as she cried, letting him draw her into his arms: a weak, limp, spent thing that loved him, but didn't know how to live with him.

"I'm so sorry," she sobbed.

After a long time, he answered, "I'm not," in a broken voice, pulling her tighter against his chest. "I'm not sorry I got the chance to love you."

They held each other and cried all the tears they had to cry, then fell asleep curled up together, clinging to each other like they couldn't bear to let go.

When Alex returned to his apartment the next night, she was gone.

He could tell because the air was dead and dark, void of her warmth. As his briefcase slipped from his hand, his other hand fluttered helplessly upward to press against his chest, which ached and throbbed as it never had before. The emptiness he felt was so sharp, it occurred to him to turn around, head to the nearest bar, get drunk, and go home with the first woman who looked at him. He'd tell her to shut up if she spoke. He'd keep her face-down beneath him. He'd bury himself inside some name-less, faceless woman and try to trick himself, for a few moments, into believing it was Jessie, that he hadn't lost her, that he wasn't alone.

Disgusted with himself for even thinking such a sick and twisted thing, he stumbled forward in the darkness to the kitchen. Taking a crystal glass out of the nearest cabinet, he poured himself a generous splash of scotch and gulped it down, pouring another glass right away.

He leaned against the counter, his heart pounding, his eyes burning. After weeks of coming home to Jessie's warmth—the TV on, dinner cooking or waiting in cheerful cartons, her body wet and pliant, grabbing for his with the same urgency with which he reached for hers, tonight was unbearable. All those blissful hours spent talking and eating and drinking and showering and fucking and making love—had he taken them for granted? Had he loved every moment as much as he should?

Throwing back the rest of his drink, he poured a third as his phone buzzed in his back pocket.

Barrett English: *What happened with Jessica?*

Alex raised the phone to throw it across the room, but stayed his hand, taking a deep, ragged breath. His hand shook as he typed two words and hit *Send*.

Alexander English: *It's over.*

He stared at the words glowing in the darkness of his kitchen, their simplicity as devastating as any tiny, efficient tool of destruction: a knife, an ice pick, the thin, deadly blade of a razor. The bright letters cut into his heart until it bled.

For the first time in Alex's empty life, during which he'd almost never been alone but always been lonely, Jessie had filled that place of bitter, desperate longing. Now that he knew how it felt to be loved, how it felt to feel full and complete, the desolation of *this* moment, standing alone in his dark, barren apartment, was more excruciating than he ever would have guessed.

He poured another splash of scotch into the glass.

How dare she walk into his world and destroy it?

He was happy before, wasn't he? Sure, the random hookups had started getting stale, and Alex conceded that watching Barrett and Fitz find their happily-ever-afters had altered something inside him. A longing had cropped up in his heart for something like they had. And he'd found it with Jessie. And in his soul he knew that it was unlikely he'd ever find it again.

He thought of Hope and Alyssa, and the multitude of other women with whom he'd been intimate over the last decade. A piece of ass here. A gratuitous fuck there. He hadn't started out wanting to hurt anyone— quite the opposite. His decision not to commit to any one woman had been intentional . . . to spare another woman from the pain that Johanna had known. How could he know that his choice to play the field meant that he would eventually end up hurting the one person he loved above any other? He raked his hands through his hair, lifting the glass to his lips again.

The doorbell to his apartment rang, and his whole body froze, wondering irrationally if it was Jessie returning to him. Racing down the hall and swinging the door open, he felt that his disappointment was complete. Barrett flinched as he watched Alex's face morph from hope to despair in the space of a moment.

"I was worried. I know how much you love her."

"Barrett," said Alex, his voice breaking.

And Alex English—the Professor, the player, the Casanova, the womanizer, the heartbreaker—whose heart had been sideswiped by a kid, who had fallen deeply in love for the first time in his life, faltered. Maybe it was the scotch, or the terrible sorrow of losing her, or the weariness he felt with his life, or the sheer emptiness that was gutting him where he stood, but his forehead dropped forward in surrender onto the solid, comforting shoulder of his big brother, who stood, grounded and certain, in silent empathy.

It was impossible that Jessie's eyes should have more tears, and yet every time she was finished crying, she would think of his smile, his soft laugh, the way his blond hair felt like silk on the back of his neck, the way it felt when she fell asleep with his chest pressed against her back . . . and she would lose it all over again.

She was wrapped in a bathrobe, sitting on the window seat in her bedroom, which overlooked the winter white of Westerly, bathed in lavender twilight. Looking past the border hedges of Westerly, she saw smoke coming from the chimneys of Haverford Park in the distance. Precious memories from her childhood and from the past five weeks meshed together, with Alex's face holding dominion.

And more tears welled up again.

A knock on her door made her quickly wipe them away, and call, "Come in."

The door opened, and Christopher peeked into the room, just his face looking around the corner of her door, and damn it if her eyes didn't burn some more.

"Tea?" he asked, a mug suddenly appearing under his chin.

"Okay," she sniffed.

Five years older than Jessie, Chris was her closest sibling, both in age and in intimacy. Unlike Brooks and Preston, who were already in college when Jessie moved to London, Cam and Chris had lived there with her and her mother for several years. After Cameron left London to attend college in the States, Jessie and Chris were the only Winslow siblings left in residence at Harrell House.

Chris was tall and broad, his thick, black hair falling in a roguish wave over his forehead and his moss-green eyes bright and vibrant. He moved gracefully across her room, holding the mug carefully so it wouldn't slosh onto the powder-pink carpet. He held it out to her, and she took it gratefully as he sat down beside her, kicking off his shoes and leaning back against the windows.

His face was severe. "What did he do to you, Jess?"

"He fell in love with me," said Jessie, bringing the mug to her lips and sipping tentatively. "And I promised him I could handle his past. I promised I could handle the women, but . . ." Her voice broke as she thought of his face last night when he said, *I think we're breaking up.* Her heart clutched, and she tried to swallow past the lump in her throat.

"You couldn't."

She shook her head.

"Well, good that you found out now," said Chris crisply, pulling a piece of lint off his sweater.

"*Good? Good?* My heart is literally breaking, Christopher. Good? There isn't anything *good* about this."

"Oh, yeah?" asked Chris, leveling his eyes at her. "Because you're here crying, talking to me, not at his place trying to figure it out."

"It can't *be* figured out."

"Everything can be figured out," said Chris simply.

"Why do you even care?" she demanded, setting the mug on the windowsill and flashing her angry eyes at him. "You four did everything possible to break us up. Why aren't you dancing a jig? Why aren't you whistling a happy tune? You can all go back to pretending your sister is some virginal sixteen-year-old!"

"I didn't want you to break up."

"You did! You—"

"Nope. The day after the squash match? You didn't get another text or call from me. Check. I'm telling the truth."

She stared back at him, thinking hard. It was *possible* that he was telling the truth.

"See, I didn't like it that you were with Alex. But then he told us that he loved you. Cam was pissed. He couldn't hear anything Alex was saying. But I could. And I could tell he was speaking from the heart. He was telling the truth. Whatever Alex did before he met you . . . well, he was a different man that afternoon. I stopped worrying about you. I stopped caring what other people thought. If Alex genuinely loved you and you genuinely loved him, it was enough for me."

Jessica drew her hands back and pushed them, as hard as possible, into her brother's chest so that he fell back, sputtering.

"What the hell, Jess?"

"Why didn't you say anything? Why didn't you do anything?"

"I did! Didn't you notice? Brooks, Pres, and Cam quit bothering you. We all agreed to stay out of it and let you live your own life."

Her mouth dropped open, and her eyes welled up again. "But I thought . . . I thought you had all given up on me. I thought you were turning your backs on me and freezing me out."

Chris shook his head. "No. You're our sister—we love you. As for Alex? We're still doing the Harrison–Lowry merger with English & Sons. Hey, I'm not going to lie—we all wish it had been anyone but Alex, but like I said, as long as he loves you and treats you right, it's none of our business."

"So you're not mad at me?"

"Just want you to be happy, Jessie. Which is why I'm sitting here . . . because I don't think I've ever seen you look quite this miserable."

"I can't move to Philly," she sobbed. "I can't live here."

"The women?"

Jessie nodded. "They're everywhere. They look at me and snicker behind my back and talk about me in whispers, waiting to see when Alex will get tired of me and move on. I can tell the ones he's been with, and it . . ."

Chris held up a hand. "Okay. I get it."

"I miss home," she said softly. "I miss my life there. I just wish I could add Alex to my life there."

"He won't go to London?"

"I think he'd leave his family for me, as much as he loves them. But not English & Sons. His career, the responsibility placed in him . . . I don't know how he could let his family down by leaving that behind. It would destroy something in him. He loves it. It's important to him."

"There are other jobs," said Chris thoughtfully.

"No," said Jess. "Not like his. Not like a company that has his name on it. Could you leave C&C Winslow? Just like that?"

Chris shook his head. "It would be tough."

Jessie picked up her mug again and took another sip.

"So that's it?" he asked. "You're just going to let him go?"

"You have no idea how hard this is. I'm fighting myself every minute not to go to him."

"He's that important to you?"

"I love him," she answered simply.

Chris bit his bottom lip in thought. "Then don't give up yet."

Jessie cocked her head to the side. She knew this look. Chris had an idea, a thought that he wasn't ready to share, but something that he was working out in his head. "Wh-what?"

Chris reached for her hand. "Don't give up on Alex yet, okay?"

She sniffled again, chuckling softly through tears. "I can't believe you just said that."

"Me neither." Chris stood, that thoughtful expression still playing across his face. He gave Jessie a quick smile before leaning down to kiss the top of her head. "Quit being so miserable. Don't forget you have four older brothers who would do almost anything to secure your happiness, Jess. It's been a long time since we all lived together, but that's never going to change. Don't ever, ever forget it."

She watched him walk purposefully to her door and leaned her head back on the wall of the window seat, letting her eyes flutter closed. When she woke up several hours later, it was pitch-dark outside, the only light coming from her phone, which had woken her up buzzing beside her, the glow brightening up the dim nook where she'd fallen asleep.

I miss you. Are you okay?–A

Her breath caught, and she bit her lip, tears welling as she stared at the words. She rubbed her eyes, still half-asleep, and answered honestly.

This hurts so much.–J
—
I love you.–A

Jessie grinned through her tears, the words beating a path to her aching heart.

Don't give up on us yet.–A
—
I love you too, but I'm leaving in three days.–J
—
I know. Just don't give up on us yet. Okay?–A

She flipped the phone over for a second, and darkness returned, thick and bleak. She hadn't given up on them, but she still didn't see a light to guide their way. Her phone buzzed, and she turned it over again.

Do you trust me?

She took a deep, ragged breath, staring at the blue letters against the bright white screen. Did she trust Alex? She searched her heart, and one searing memory cut through all the others. It felt like yesterday when she had looked up at twelve-year-old Alex's bright blue eyes as he chucked her under the chin and handed her an extra flashlight, announcing to the crowd of older kids who'd told her to get lost, "She's on *my* team." His voice had dared any of them to contradict him, but no one had. Then, as now, despite the time, despite the distance, despite everything that had happened between them, Jessie was still on Alex's team.

Always.

His reply was instantaneous.

Then I'll see you tomorrow.

She felt a little deflated, and her body, which hadn't spent a night away from Alex for over three weeks, felt deprived and frustrated as she drew her knees to her chest. Like he could read her mind all the way from Rittenhouse Square, his next message arrived with uncanny precision.

Don't get used to sleeping without me, Jess.

She gasped, and the first and only smile of the day burst across her face as she touched her fingers to the words, thinking that it would take something much stronger than a day apart to ever stop wanting Alex English beside her in bed.

Chapter 13

Christmas Eve dawned gray and rainy, a fine complement to Alex's mood after sleeping alone for the first time in weeks. But he consoled himself that if everything went according to plan today, he'd have Jessica back in his life by tonight and he never intended to spend another night away from her, ever again.

Barrett had stayed for hours last night, listening to Alex talk about his life, the many women he'd sampled and enjoyed, the way he'd felt when Barrett and Fitz got engaged, and how Jessie had come along at the perfect moment and filled the void in his life. He talked about Jessie as a child, wide-eyed and trusting, and as an adult, sweet yet determined, trusting and bold, the missing piece of his life, the most fun he'd ever had. He told Barrett how easy it was to fall in love with her, how helpless he was to stop it, how much he needed Jessie in his life now that he could compare his life before her with his life after. He raged against the partnership that bound him to English & Sons, even as he contradicted himself by admitting how much the company meant to him.

And all the while, Barrett listened and offered advice, even going so far as to say that English & Sons would hire a new CFO if Alex needed to follow Jessie to London, as long as he stayed on long enough for a smooth transition. But Alex winced at the idea. From the cradle, Barrett, Fitz, Alex, Stratton, and Weston had been grown and groomed to take over their father's company. The idea of walking away from it sat like lead in Alex's belly, almost as heavy as the idea of letting Jessie go.

It wasn't until nine o'clock, when Barrett's phone rang, that they'd taken a break from their conversation. His face didn't soften as it did when Emily called; it was stern and fixed, thoughtful and silent, processing whatever information was being relayed. At one point, Barrett turned around and fixed his glance on Alex, narrowing his eyes and nodding.

After listening for a long time, he finally nodded, rubbing his jaw. "I see the benefits. It's an interesting idea, I agree. Tomorrow. At noon."

As Barrett pocketed his phone and turned to Alex, he finally took off his suit jacket and loosened his tie.

"I hope you have nowhere you need to be tonight. Call Stratton and tell him to get over here. We have some work to do."

Five hours later, Barrett left for Emily's warm bed, and Alex headed to his own cold, lonesome room, albeit with a lighter heart than earlier in the evening. He sat on the edge of the bed where he'd made love to Jess more times than he could count, and texted how much he missed her.

As morning light filtered through the window, Alex took a deep breath, burying his face in her pillow, his heart swelling when the smell of tea roses greeted him.

Though English & Sons was closed for business on Christmas Eve, Alex had an important meeting in the conference room at noon. But before that meeting, he had a couple of other very important errands to run. Whipping the sheet off his naked body, he stalked to the shower, promising himself that no matter what happened by the end of today, he would live with the consequences. Oh, but what hope surged through him, as he promised every power of the universe that if he got her back, he'd spend the rest of his life making sure he was worthy of her.

Jessica sat in front of the fireplace in a forest-green cocktail dress, sipping a glass of champagne, as her mother, Brooks, and Preston decorated the Christmas tree in the living room of Westerly. Every Christmas since she was nine years old had been spent at Harrell House in London, and Jessie felt out of step at Westerly this year. Or maybe it was just that she felt out of step without Alex, whose absence was a constant heaviness on her heart.

Since her exchanged texts with him last night, she hadn't heard from him again. Christopher and Cameron had gone into the office for most of the afternoon—a decision that sent their mother into a fit—and returned about an hour ago, rushing upstairs to get ready for Christmas Eve dinner.

Tomorrow was Christmas, and the day after, Jessie would fly back to London. She'd spent most of today crying as she packed up her belongings, whatever hopes Alex had raised with his messages last night dying slowly over the course of another day without him. Did she trust him? Yes. But had he given her a reason—any reason—to hold on? Sadly, no.

Catching Brooks's eyes from across the room, she watched him hand an ornament to his mother and cross the room to sit beside her.

"How's my girl?"

"She's sad," Jessie said softly, grateful that it finally appeared she'd run out of tears.

"It's Christmas Eve," said Brooks. "Don't magical things happen on Christmas Eve?"

"When we were little, Dad would play Santa on Christmas Eve."

Brooks chuckled softly. "I remember, but I'm surprised you do, kid."

"Mom painted his black mustache with white shoe polish. And by the time the older kids took their turns on his lap, it would flake off on their shoulders."

Brooks nodded at her with wonder. "That's right. You have some memory."

"They aren't my memories. They're Alex's."

Brooks's expression cooled, and he looked away from Jess, toward the fire. "We didn't want you to get hurt, Jess."

"I got hurt anyway."

"I'm sorry if I had anything to do with that," said Brooks. "I just want what's best for you. I always have."

"I know," she said, giving him a small, sad smile. "And I love you for it."

"*And* you love Alex."

"Yes."

"I heard he asked you to stay."

"He did."

"But you won't?"

"I can't." She looked down at her glass, which she rolled between her palms slowly. "All day today, I've thought to myself: If you really loved Alex, nothing could keep you apart. If you really loved him, you'd stay."

Brooks raised his eyebrows, waiting for her to continue.

"But I love more than Alex. I love what Alex and I are when we're together. And if I stayed, I wouldn't be protecting that. Because little by little, I wouldn't be the person he fell in love with anymore. I'd change into someone different. Someone suspicious and unhappy and defensive." She took a deep breath, then exhaled in a rush through her lips. "Does that make sense?"

"It's not worth the chance?"

"The chance of destroying the love we have for each other?" She shook her head. "Nothing's worth that, Brooks. Compromising is good. It's important to bend for someone you love. But too much compromising means breaking, means I'm not being true to myself or protecting the love I have for him."

"Okay." Brooks sighed, letting the matter drop, and they sat in silence for a few minutes, watching the logs in the fireplace snap and crackle. "It was nice having you here, Jess. I'll miss you when you go back."

"You've barely seen me this visit," she said, pursing her lips. "And when you did, you were mostly mad at me."

He laughed quietly. "Maybe so . . . but you managed to make your point. You're all grown up. I won't stand in your way again."

The doorbell rang, and Jessie's forehead creased in confusion as she looked at her mother, who placed a final decoration on the Christmas tree before clapping her hands together and smiling at Jess.

"Our guests are here!"

"G-guests?" she asked, smoothing out the skirt of her dress.

"Oh, didn't I tell you? It must have slipped my mind, and you were locked in your room packing all day. Eleanora was kind enough to have us for Thanksgiving. It seemed only right to have the English and Edwards families join us for Christmas Eve."

Alex stepped through the front door with his family, into the front hallway at Westerly, just in time to see Cameron and

Christopher coming down the stairs, freshly showered and dressed properly for Christmas Eve dinner. Olivia Winslow greeted them all with hugs and kisses as two maids took their coats, and Brooks and Preston rounded the corner of the large drawing room to the left, standing side by side and staring at Alex.

As Olivia ushered the Edwardses and Tom and Eleanora English into the drawing room for cocktails, the nine brothers lingered. Chris and Cam crossed the vestibule to stand with Brooks and Preston, across from Barrett, Fitz, Alex, Stratton, and Wes. They were all waiting to see what would happen next, to see if the hatchet was finally buried.

After a moment, Brooks stepped forward, offering his hand to Alex. Alex took it, and Brooks leaned forward, whispering, "If you mess this up, I'll hunt you down, English."

Alex stepped back, nodding gravely before shaking hands with Preston, too, then Cam and Chris. The mood lightened, but still there was no sign of Jessica. As the men turned toward the drawing room, Christopher held back, staring at Alex.

"Where is she?" asked Alex.

"Pres said she went up the back stairs as soon as she heard you were coming."

Alex flinched. "She doesn't want to see me?"

"She loves you. My guess is that she can't bear to say good-bye again."

"You and Cam didn't tell her?"

Christopher shrugged. "We figured that was up to you."

"I don't know how to thank you, Chris," said Alex, "for thinking up the whole plan and calling Barrett last night."

"She's my sister. I'm not just going to let her be miserable if I see a solution. Even if the solution includes you." Chris said this with attitude, but a slight smile softened the words at the end.

Alex nodded, glancing at the stairs, then back at Chris.

Chris's lips tightened, and he shook his head back and forth. "I can't believe I'm about to give Alex English directions to my sister's bedroom."

Alex grinned. "I heard he's turning over a new leaf."

"He better be," said Chris. "Or he's not getting out of this house alive."

"Where is she?"

"Two flights up. At the top of the stairs, turn left. Hers is the room at the end of the hall." Chris checked his watch. "I'm guessing you have about half an hour before dinner."

"You were always my favorite Winslow, Chris," said Alex, slapping him on the shoulder before taking the stairs two at a time.

Alex is here. Alex is downstairs.

Still holding her half-full champagne flute with trembling fingers, she paced in the dim light of her room, finally stopping in front of the window. Her eyes burned with new tears, and her chest ached so much, she could almost feel her heart breaking. She'd spent the last four weeks hiding *with* Alex. Now she was hiding *from* him.

She tried to take a deep breath, but she couldn't.

What was her mother thinking? She knew how painful this separation from Alex was for Jess. She knew that Jess was hanging on by the skin of her teeth, counting the minutes until she boarded the plane back for London. How was she supposed to sit through cocktails and dinner with the source of her joy, the source of her pain?

Taking a shaking breath, she sat down on the window seat, feeling lost and confused. From the moment she saw Alex walk into Cameron's apartment building, all she'd wanted was him. No, that wasn't true. She rewound her life much further, to her childhood, to Alex's lips brushing her forehead as she anticipated another journey to London with just as heavy a heart. What would her nine-year-old self say to her now, she wondered, as she walked away from a chance with Alex just because she couldn't handle his past?

His past.

"His *past*," she said aloud, wincing as she really listened to the word. Past. Over. Gone. Finished.

And suddenly she realized, the women he'd been with were just remnants of his past. Wistful for something over. Devotees of something gone. Reaching for something already finished. Someday someone stronger than Jessie would stare them down, hold her head high, and, yes, even feel sorry for them as she walked forward, into the future, with Alex, leaving them all behind.

And that someone wouldn't be Jessie, because she would have already run away.

Her breath caught as her words to him so long ago—*our experiences help shape who we are, but they don't define us*—came back to haunt her. How had she lost sight of that? She'd allowed a handful (okay, in fairness, a very *large* handful) of bitter, jealous women to define them. Instead of defining her relationship with Alex in terms of a future together, she'd wallowed in his past, allowing his experiences to define it for her. Somewhere along the way, she'd lost sight of what mattered, of what she truly wanted.

For all its comforts and familiarity, she knew in her heart that London without Alex would be excruciating. Anywhere she was without Alex would make her homesick because the only home her heart would acknowledge was with him.

She stood and wiped her eyes, slugging down the rest of her champagne. She still didn't love the idea of relocating. But she took a deep breath and pulled up her big-girl panties.

If he'd still have her, it was time for her to reclaim what belonged to her.

With a determined nod, she placed her glass on the vanity and turned toward her bedroom door. Someone rapped on the door just as she reached it, and swinging it open, expecting to see Chris or her mother, she felt the wind knocked out of her as what belonged to her was suddenly standing directly in front of her.

"Where are you headed?" asked Alex, drinking in the beloved, welcome sight of Jessie after two days and one lonesome night of stark deprivation. Tea rose enveloped him, and he fought to keep his eyes open, and to not reach for her instantly.

"Downstairs," she whispered in a breathless voice.

"Could we talk up here for a minute?" he asked, sidling into her room and closing the door behind him. He leaned against it, dying to reach for her, but uncertain of their footing. The last thing he wanted to do was anything that would push her away further.

Her breasts heaved against the dark fabric of her dress with every breath, and her face, so lovely in the moonlight, looked tired. But despite the telltale puffiness around her eyes, he was surprised to see a little spark of spirit in them too. The despair, the sorrowful surrender, from two nights ago wasn't there anymore.

He was glad, but at the same time his heart fell. Had she already started moving on from their short love affair? Looking forward to her life in London and leaving him behind?

"Sure," she said, walking across the room to the long, plush window seat that spanned the entire wall and gave her a bird's-eye view of Westerly and Haverford Park beyond.

She sat down, gesturing to the seat with her hand. Her fingers fluttered. Just a slight tremble, but his heart surged with hope.

"How are you?" he asked, sitting down beside her.

"I've been better," she answered. "I was coming downstairs to find you."

"You were? I thought you came up here to escape me."

"I needed a minute," she confessed.

Staring at her profile, his heart swelled and burned with love for her, uncomfortable, fierce, desperate.

"I love you," he whispered.

Her breath caught, and her eyes fluttered as she turned to face him. "I love you too."

His shoulders slumped in relief, and he reached for her waist, drawing her into his arms and kissing her frantically. His lips sealed, possessive and greedy, over hers, his tongue seeking hers. He felt the wild thumping of her heart against his chest as she moaned softly, flattening her hands over his shirt. She was Jess, and she was his, and he was never letting her go again.

"The last two days were hell," he murmured, settling his forehead in the curve of her neck and dropping his lips to her skin where they rested, as though finally home.

"Worse," she agreed.

"I'm not doing that ever again."

"Me neither."

He leaned back, searching her eyes. "No?"

Jessie shook her head, her trapped hands sliding up his chest to cradle his cheeks. "No." She swallowed, summoning her courage. "I'll stay."

"What?"

"I'll stay," she said again, stronger this time. "I'm so sorry I let it get to me."

"No, Jess," he said softly. "I'm so sorry I lived my life in such a way that it ended up hurting you."

"I'm not losing you, Alex. I'm not giving up what we have. You're more important to me than anything else. I'll stay in Philadelphia."

He placed his hands over hers, lacing his fingers through hers. "I can't let you do that, baby."

She whimpered, a sound of pain launching from the back of her throat. "But you said the last two days were hell. You said you weren't doing that ever again."

"I'm not. I love you, Jess. I'm not letting you go . . . without me."

"Without you? To England?"

He drew back from her, holding up a hand. "Wait. Let me explain, okay? It's a little more complicated than that. But I think it's our chance, Jess, if you'll take it with me."

Alex took her hands in his, letting them fall on the cushion between them. Her mind was whirling, but any conversation that started with love and included a chance to be together was a conversation she wanted to have. She squeezed his fingers, urging him to continue.

"It was Christopher's idea," he said, searching her face. "You know how we're doing a deal with your brothers? It's a shipbuilding merger. English & Sons has acquired Harrison Shipbuilding, which is located on the North Shore of Long Island in New York, and your brothers are in the process of buying Lowry Shipbuilding near Devon, on the southwest coast of England. Then we'll merge the two companies together and have an international shipbuilding company with manufacturing in the U.S. and England."

"I know this. Chris told me about it a few weeks ago, when I first arrived."

"For a deal like this, you need someone to act as a project manager. That person sort of, well, commutes between the locations for a little while, managing the transition from two smaller companies to one larger one. In terms of this deal, it means someone who spends a few weeks in the Hamptons, a few weeks in Devon, and a few weeks in Philly over the course of the next year."

"Chris is that person," she said. "I know he wasn't crazy about it at first, but my mother loves the idea of seeing him more often while he's working in Devon."

He squeezed her hands. "Your mother's going to be disappointed, then."

"Why?" she asked, still not seeing where he was going with this.

She'd heard their roles outlined several times, both by Alex and her brothers: Cam and Alex were the CFOs, the money—they had to stay in Philly. Barrett and Fitz had personal obligations, which left Chris or Stratton. Chris had balked at first because it meant that he and Cam couldn't take on new deals while he was managing the merger, but he'd eventually consented because Stratton was so opposed to the travel. So what did he mean?

"Did you know that Stratton is a CPA?"

"No."

"He is. He's younger than I am by a few years, but almost any financial work I do, I pass by Strat first. He's practically a wizard with numbers."

"Stratton doesn't want to go to England."

"But I do."

"Oh no. No, Alex! No." Her eyes widened and brightened as she finally understood what he'd done for her. "You resigned as CFO. You resigned from English & Sons."

"Sort of." His smile was sweet and certain, heartbreaking in its hope and poignancy. "I resigned as CFO, but not from English & Sons. As of this afternoon, Stratton is the new CFO, and I'm the new vice president of new business, mergers, and acquisitions for English & Sons."

She unclasped his hand, covering her gasp with her palm as tears welled from her eyes, spilling over the sides and trailing down her cheeks.

"Jess . . . ," Alex murmured in a voice full of love, pulling her back into his arms and rubbing her back with gentle strokes. "Jess, I'm no good without you. You fill this deep ache inside me. You make me a better man. You make me good. You make me whole."

"Alex," she sobbed.

The depth of his love made her tremble, made her heart burst, made her feel humble and profoundly grateful. He'd changed his entire life for her—he'd given up his social life, and now his job and his home. For her. All for her.

"I'll have to travel to wherever the business takes me, but you could come with me everywhere I go, Jess. You could still keep your apartment in London, and I'll still keep mine here, but we'll globe-trot together. A few weeks in England, a few in New York, Philly now and then . . . who knows where else as we take on more projects? A few weeks in China, in Chile, in France. The only permanent home we'll have for a while is each other. Could you live like that for a few years? With me?"

The excitement of it flushed her cheeks as she imagined a few weeks with Alex in an apartment near Montmartre, in a hotel suite that overlooked the Andes, the whole world their playground as they traveled together to exotic places, touching down in London or Philadelphia only long enough to recharge their batteries and reconnect with family. He was offering her the chance of a lifetime on a silver platter. With him. Her heart clenched and raced with love and wonder that two days ago their future should look so bleak, and now . . . so possible.

"It sounds like the best adventure ever," she said, smiling at him through tears, giggling as he pressed his forehead to hers.

"Is that a yes?"

"Yes!"

He tilted his head, and his lips caught hers, tugging at the top one. As he pulled her tighter against him, she knew—she *knew*—that there was nothing Alex wouldn't do to make her happy. His tongue swirled around hers, distracting her from her thoughts as her body pushed up against his, the burn in her tummy begging her to lie back, spread her legs, and urge him forward to soothe the ache, to quench the thirst, to requite the longing that only Alex could relieve.

He surprised her by pulling away. His eyes were almost wild, searching hers in the moonlight that streamed in through the windows.

"You trust me, Jess?"

"Always," she answered, without hesitation.

"As long as you're handing out yeses, I'm going to press my luck," he said, drawing back from her and slipping to the floor on one knee.

She gasped. "What are you doing?"

"Just listen," he said, taking one of her hands in his.

The moonlight shone upon his face as his tongue lashed out quickly to wet his lips, a gesture she'd come to recognize as nerves. She tried to calm the fierce beating of her heart by taking a deep, shaky breath and smiling at him.

"Jess, since the moment you walked back into my life, everything's changed. How I see the world. How I see myself. What I want. Who I want it with. You're my reason for everything. There's literally nothing I wouldn't do for you. Do you know that?"

She bit her bottom lip as tears coursed down her cheeks. "I know that now."

"I promise to treat you with kindness and respect every day of my life.

"Anytime you need to laugh, I'll roll out the worst pickup lines I can think of.

"I must be smart because I choose to do whatever it takes to be with you, and I don't know how interesting I am, but we're planning to travel a lot, so that'll broaden my horizons.

"How about we be daring in bed because we're pretty good at that already? And I'm hoping with every ounce of strength in my body that, right here, right now, me on my knees looking up at you is a good surprise.

"I know your toes curl when I kiss you because I've felt them curl against mine.

"And speaking of those toes, when they're cold, I'll always be ready to warm them up.

"I promise I will never, ever look away, Jess, because I'll never look at anyone else but you.

"I choose you, Jess. Only you.

"If you'll have me."

Alex let go of her hand, reached into his breast pocket, and pulled out a simple solitaire-diamond ring, which he held up to her. Catching a moonbeam through the window, the facets sparkled, glowing between his fingers.

His eyes, bright with emotion, captured hers, and he chuckled lightly before settling into a confident smile. "And though I have *loved* being your boyfriend, it's time for the whole world to know that Alex English is absolutely, positively off the market forever.

"I love you, Jessica Fairchild Winslow. Will you be my wife?"

It occurred to her halfway through his beautiful proposal that he was echoing everything she'd said she wanted that first night on the balcony of the Union League Club. And how Jessie had managed to sit still, and not throw her arms around him, was a mystery for the ages.

As tears coursed down her cheeks, she nodded at Alex, swallowing the lump in her throat just enough to say, "Yes" and hold out a trembling hand. He slid the gorgeous ring onto her finger and raised it to his lips, kissing her finger first, then the soft pillow at the base of her thumb, the bone on the side of her wrist, and finally the middle of her palm.

"Because you missed these kisses this morning," he whispered. "Because I'll never miss another day again."

Jessica's laughter mixed with tears of joy as she fell to her knees beside him, wrapping her arms around his neck. Now that Alex belonged to her, she had no intention of ever letting him go.

There used to be something *wrong* with Alex English.
Until one day, he met the *right* girl.
And all of his dreams came true.

THE END

The English Brothers continues with . . .

SEDUCED BY STRATTON

THE ENGLISH BROTHERS, BOOK #4

THE ENGLISH BROTHERS
(Part I of the Blueberry Lane Series)

Breaking Up with Barrett
Falling for Fitz
Anyone but Alex
Seduced by Stratton
Wild about Weston
Kiss Me Kate
Marrying Mr. English

Turn the page to read a sneak peek of *Seduced by Stratton*!

Chapter 1

Stratton English knew what his brothers said about him.

"I don't think he's ever had a girlfriend." (Barrett)

"I don't think he's ever had sex." (Alex)

"He always friend-zones himself." (Fitz)

"He's just not smooth around women." (Weston)

It often occurred to Stratton to set them straight—tell Barrett he'd had a couple of girlfriends in college, though they didn't last very long. While he was at it, he'd tell reformed lothario Alex that, while he'd had sex, he wasn't in the habit of sleeping around. Smiling affectionately as he thought of his favorite brother, Fitz, he'd have to agree that he had a problem with being friend-zoned, and while Weston was right in general, being incredibly awkward around women wasn't the primary reason Stratton was single.

The simple fact was this:

His heart was already taken.

Hearing a sound from the hallway, he peeked out the peephole of his apartment door again, but the corridor was empty. Tamping down his disappointment, he straightened his glasses and walked back into the living room. He sat in the easy chair by the fireplace, picked up his Kindle, and

took a sip of Merlot before settling into his latest self-help
book.

"Latest" because he'd read them all:
How to Seduce the Girl of Your Dreams
Seduction for Dummies
1-2-3 Seduce Me!
The Blueprint for Seduction
Deduce to Seduce
This evening's choice was called *Ten Steps to Seduction*,
and Stratton didn't feel especially hopeful about the advice.
Then again, as he waited for the elevator to ding, followed
by the sound of Amy fumbling with her keys two doors
down, he might as well keep busy.

Amy Colson. Amy. He took a deep breath, picturing her
face.

Stratton had moved into his apartment almost two years
ago on a chilly March day, annoyed that his movers had to
share the service elevator with those of another tenant moving in. All day his things had arrived in spurts while his
movers alternated elevator runs, and by six o'clock he was
irritated that it was taking so long.

That is, until *she* knocked on his door.

Dressed in sweat pants and an old UPenn T-shirt that
had seen better days, Stratton had stood in the doorway
of his new apartment, staring at the young woman who'd
suddenly appeared on his doorstep.

"Mr. English?" she asked.

Her blonde hair was straight, just touching her shoulders, and her blue eyes were bright. She was small and fit,
and he knew she would be considered conventionally pretty,
but good looks were mostly lost on Stratton. Unlike every
other man in the world, he almost always became attracted
to a woman's personality first, her looks second. His mother
called him "immune to women's wiles."

"Yes?"

The metal bracelets she wore clinked together not unpleasantly as she gestured down the hall to the left, and then held out her hand in greeting. "I'm Amy Colson. From next door."

"Next door is Mrs. Dorchester."

"Oh." Amy Colson gave him a look, as if trying to figure out if he was teasing. Then she chuckled, her hand still dangling awkwardly between them. "Right. You're very precise! I'm actually *two* doors down."

"You're the other new tenant," said Stratton, finally noticing her hand. He rushed to shake it, grasping it too hard in his haste, and she winced, pulling away.

"Yeah." Glancing down, she rubbed her hands together before looking up at his shirt. "Did you go? To Penn?"

"No," he answered.

"Oh. Do you work there?"

"No."

"Huh." She raised her eyebrows and grinned. "Are you pulling my leg?"

"No," he answered, crossing his arms over his chest.

"Just found that shirt lying around and put it on, huh?"

"No. It was a gift."

"Oh." She shrugged. "Okay."

Amy Colson looked away, her smile fading as her cheeks grew pink, and Stratton knew he'd just done it again. He felt nervous, giving her monosyllabic answers, and making things awkward.

Her little, pink tongue darted out to lick her lips as she pushed her hair back, and Stratton found himself distracted by the perfect shell of her ear. It looked delicate, yet soft, architecturally perfect like the inner curve of a conch, and he stared at it for an extra second before looking back at her face.

"Are you an ear-guy?" she asked with a little grin.

"I don't know what that is."

"You know, some guys love the eyes, some love the . . . the . . ." She took a deep breath and pushed her chest out a little, cocking her head to the side.

"Lungs?"

Amy Colson stared back at him, her brows knitting together. "N-No. Not the lungs, the um . . ."

She bent her head meaningfully toward him and searched his eyes like they were engaging in telepathy.

"I can't hear your thoughts," he blurted out, knowing as soon as he said it how ridiculous it sounded.

Her eyebrows had merged into one V-shaped unibrow and two little wrinkles appeared at the top of her nose— almost like a scowl, but more confused. She quirked her head to the side, rubbing her bottom lip with her finger.

"Can you hear *other people's* thoughts?"

"Absolutely not. That was a stupid thing to say, I just . . ." *I don't know how to talk to girls, and you're making me nervous.*

Her eyebrows relaxed, and she nodded thoughtfully.

"Hey, I know!" She gave him a sweet smile. "Can we start over?"

This was interesting to Stratton. He'd realized several minutes ago he and Amy Colson were in the midst of a very awkward conversation, but he didn't know what to do about it. A "do-over" seemed like an excellent idea, and the suggestion made him relax . . . and warm toward her considerably.

"Okay," he agreed softly.

She turned around, walked four steps away, then pivoted and walked back to Stratton with a big grin. When she stopped at his door and held out her hand, Stratton shook it lightly right away, and noticed it was small and warm, her skin soft against his.

"Hi. I'm Amy Colson," she said, her teeth white and straight and very perfect. "I just moved in two doors down."

"I'm Stratton English," he answered, realizing, for the first time, what an unusual and striking shade of blue her eyes were. "I moved in today too."

"You're one of the English brothers. From Haverford."

"Yes. Have we met?"

"Aside from five minutes ago? No," she said, withdrawing her hand gently from his, and Stratton was surprised by how sorry he was to feel it go. "But I know your brother Weston a little from the Hunt Club. And I've met Alex."

"Everyone's met Alex."

She chuckled lightly, and her cheeks flushed pink. "I haven't *met* Alex . . . like *that*."

He liked the sound of her laugh. It wasn't high and grating—it was low and breathy. It made his heart beat a little faster.

"So, we're neighbors now," she said. "And you didn't go to UPenn, and you don't read minds."

He smiled, grateful for how she'd salvaged their first introduction. His heart fluttered a little as he realized he liked her. He took a step forward, leaning against the doorjamb. Channeling Alex's suaveness as best he could, he gathered his courage to ask, "Amy Colson, want to share a pizza?"

As a rule, Stratton's dating life wasn't very robust. Although set up by his brothers now and then, he'd had few girlfriends of his own, likely owing to the fact that he had what Barrett called "no filter." Especially when he was nervous, Stratton said the first thing that popped into his head, which wasn't always the most popular or appropriate thing to share. He'd mostly learned to keep his thoughts to himself, except around his brothers. But girls were still a mystery to him for whom he longed and by whom he was terrified. Still, Amy Colson, with humor and gentleness, had given him a second chance, and if he believed in love at first sight, Stratton would have acknowledged he'd just fallen victim to it.

The elevator behind them dinged, and before she answered, Amy turned to look as the doors opened. A tall, dark-haired, good-looking man craned his neck, looking back and forth down the hallway before glimpsing Amy and flashing her a perfect smile. Stratton's heart dropped like it was tethered to stone. It was Étienne Rousseau.

With his eyes glued to Amy, Étienne sauntered over, grabbed her around the waist, hauled her against his body, and kissed her passionately. Instead of looking away, Stratton stared, fascinated, as Amy moaned, wrapping her soft, warm hands around Étienne's neck. Stratton's own body tightened with arousal and jealousy, and he took a step back into his apartment, jerking his head down, surprised by the strength of his feelings.

"Oh! Ten. Ten, stop," Amy said in a breathy voice, giggling as she pulled away from him. "You have to meet Stratton, my new neighbor."

Étienne kissed Amy's nose, then looked at Stratton, offering a pretentious smirk. "English."

"Rousseau."

"Wait! You know each other?" asked Amy.

Know each other? We sure do, thought Stratton derisively.

Not only did Étienne Rousseau deflower Stratton's cousin, Kate English, a few weeks after her fifteenth birthday, when she was visiting Haverford Park with her parents over spring break, but he'd bragged about it all over St. Michael's Academy. And yes, Alex, who was a senior at the time, had eventually kicked sophomore Étienne's ass in the front courtyard after morning mass one sunny April day, but it hadn't been enough as far as Stratton was concerned. Étienne had hurt Kate. He had disappointed and disrespected her. Further, he was a self-absorbed egomaniac and didn't care about anyone

but himself. Stratton would go so far to say that he hated
Étienne Rousseau.

The object of his disdain still had his arm possessively
around Amy's waist. He pulled her against his side, kissing
her temple while holding Stratton's eyes with that mock-
ing, supercilious expression. "Your *new* neighbor is my *old*
neighbor, *chérie*."

"We grew up on the same street," Stratton explained,
crossing his arms over his chest and eyeing Étienne with
distaste.

"How's your cousin?" asked Étienne, licking his lips
slowly.

Stratton sneered and took a step forward, but Amy's
happy voice stopped him.

"How great!" exclaimed Amy. "We're all friends, and
Stratton just invited us for pizza."

Us? No way he'd have invited Étienne.

"N-No, I—"

"My guess is that he asked *you* for pizza, *petite*," said Étienne with a cocky smirk. "Thanks for the invite, but Amy
doesn't like pizza. I'm taking her out for a *real* dinner."

For a moment, Stratton's thoughts lingered on how
unimaginable it was that Amy didn't like pizza. But he was
soon distracted by Étienne leaning down to kiss her again,
pulling her body flush against his, and kneading his fingers
into her ass as he pillaged her mouth. Étienne executed all
of this right in front of Stratton in a way that was meant to
establish possession, with zero regard or respect for Amy,
and Stratton's fists curled at his sides as he watched.

When Amy drew back she was flushed and breathless,
and Stratton's fingers unfurled, helplessly undone by the
softness of her face. All he could think was he wished it was
him who'd made her look that way. And damn it, he wished
he'd known she was dating Étienne *Slimeball* Rousseau

before he met her. He clenched his teeth when she looked at him with her beautiful, cerulean-blue eyes.

"Rain check?" she asked him with an impish grin, taking Étienne's hand.

"Sure," mumbled Stratton, watching as they walked down the hall, stopping by the elevator to kiss again. It made him ache to have met such an amazing girl, only to find out she was taken by a douchebag. They stepped onto the elevator, but at the last minute Amy darted out, caught his eyes and given him a quick wave. It was that little wave that secured his fate. Whatever it took . . . whatever he had to do . . . he would fix this. He would find a way to pry Amy away from Étienne. He would save her, as he hadn't been able to save Kate so long ago.

Look for *Seduced by Stratton* at your local bookstore or buy online!

Other Books by Katy Regnery

A MODERN FAIRYTALE
(Stand-alone, full-length, unconnected romances inspired by classic fairy tales.)

The Vixen and the Vet
(inspired by "Beauty and the Beast")
2014

Never Let You Go
(inspired by "Hansel and Gretel")
2015

Ginger's Heart
(inspired by "Little Red Riding Hood")
2016

Don't Speak
(inspired by "The Little Mermaid")
2017

Swan Song
(inspired by "The Ugly Duckling")
2018

ENCHANTED PLACES
(Stand-alone, full-length stories that are set in beautiful places.)

Playing for Love at Deep Haven
2015

Restoring Love at Bolton Castle
2016

Risking Love at Moonstone Manor
2017

A Season of Love at Summerhaven
2018

ABOUT THE AUTHOR

USA Today **bestselling author Katy Regnery** started her writing career by enrolling in a short story class in January 2012. One year later, she signed her first contract for a winter romance entitled *By Proxy*.

Katy claims authorship of the multi-titled Blueberry Lane Series which follows the English, Winslow, Rousseau, Story and Ambler families of Philadelphia, the five-book, best-selling A Modern Fairytale series, the Enchanted Places series, and a standalone novella, *Frosted*.

Katy's first Modern Fairytale romance, *The Vixen and the Vet,* was nominated for a RITA® in 2015 and won the 2015 Kindle Book Award for romance. Four of her books: *The Vixen and the Vet* (A Modern Fairytale), *Never Let You Go* (A Modern Fairytale), *Falling for Fitz* (The English Brothers #2) and *By Proxy* (Heart of Montana #1) have been #1 genre bestsellers on Amazon. Katy's boxed set, The English Brothers Boxed Set, Books #1–4, hit the *USA Today* bestseller list in 2015 and her Christmas story, *Marrying Mr. English*, appeared on the same list a week later.

Katy lives in the relative wilds of northern Fairfield County, Connecticut, where her writing room looks out at the woods, and her husband, two young children, and two dogs create just enough cheerful chaos to remind her that the very best love stories begin at home.

Sign up for Katy's newsletter today: http://www.katyregnery.com!

Connect with Katy

Katy LOVES connecting with her readers and answers every e-mail, message, tweet, and post personally! Connect with Katy!

Katy's Website: http://katyregnery.com
Katy's E-mail: katy@katyregnery.com
Katy's Facebook Page: https://www.facebook.com/KatyRegnery
Katy's Pinterest Page: https://www.pinterest.com/
   katharineregner
Katy's Amazon Profile: http://www.amazon.com/
   Katy-Regnery/e/B00FDZKXYU
Katy's Goodreads Profile: https://www.goodreads.com/author/
   show/7211470.Katy_Regnery

CPSIA information can be obtained at www.ICGtesting.com
Printed in the USA
LVOW11s0355200416

484247LV00004B/5/P